ENJOY ALL OF THE BOOKS IN
THE GUARDIANS *of* GA'HOOLE SERIES!

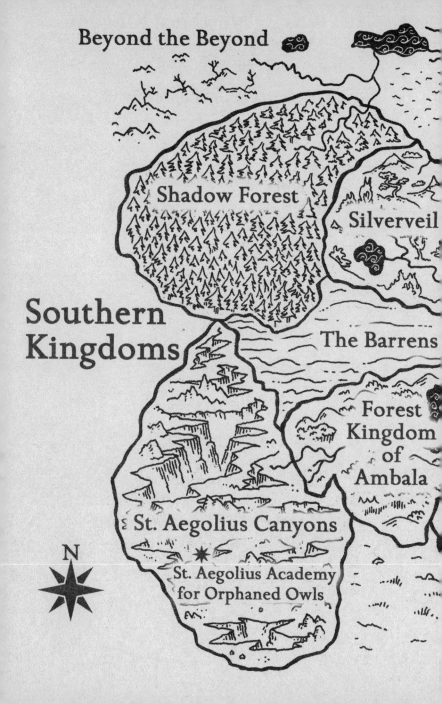

Broken Talon Point

Northern Kingdoms

Peninsula
of the
Spirit Woods

Ice
Narrows

Sea of Hoolemere

Cape
Glaux

Island of Hoole

The Beaks

Desert
of
Kuneer

Forest Kingdom
of Tyto

Soren's Hollow

River Hoole

The wolves stood back as Hamish came forward and tucked in next to Coryn on the hindquarter. "I'm not used to this much meat. I mostly gnaw bones."

"So I've heard," Coryn replied.

GUARDIANS
of GA'HOOLE

BOOK EIGHT

The Outcast

BY KATHRYN LASKY

SCHOLASTIC INC.

New York Toronto London Auckland Sydney
Mexico City New Delhi Hong Kong Buenos Aires

No part of this publication may be reproduced, or stored in a retrieval system, or transmitted in any form or by any means, electronic, mechanical, photocopying, recording, or otherwise, without written permission of the publisher. For information regarding permission, write to Scholastic Inc., Attention: Permissions Department, 557 Broadway, New York, NY 10012.

ISBN 0-439-73951-9

Text copyright © 2005 by Kathryn Lasky. All rights reserved. Published by Scholastic Inc. SCHOLASTIC and associated logos are trademarks and/or registered trademarks of Scholastic Inc.

Artwork by Richard Cowdrey
Design by Steve Scott

12 11 10 9 8 7 6 5 4   7 8 9 10/0

Printed in the U.S.A.   40

First printing, September 2005

Northern Kingdoms

N

Glauxian Brothers
Retreat

Bitter
Sea

Kiel Bay

Stormfast Island

Bay of Fangs

Everwinter Sea

Ice Talons

Ice
Narrows

Dark Fowl Island

Southern
Kingdoms

Contents

Prologue

"You are a mask. You are nothing more! There is nothing behind your mask, not a face, nothing! I shall fly in the fullness of the night. Under the moon and the stars I shall hunt the vole, the rat, even the fox. I shall become part of owlkind, no matter where I have to go. But I shall go! And I shall never ever return to the Pure Ones. I defy you. I HAVE FREE WILL!"

Shouting, Nyroc flew directly at the mask that hung over the still water of the small lake. It was the mask of his father's scroom, Kludd, who had haunted him ever since Nyroc had fled the Pure Ones. And now the glaring mask seemed to grow dim and tarnished. Silently, it shattered. Shards of the once-burnished metal that had hidden Kludd's war-mangled face fell without a splash into the water. Nary a ripple disturbed the placid surface of the pond.

Gone? Is he gone at last? It seemed too good to be true. Once, twice, three times Nyroc flew over the lake, peering into its amber depths, but all the young owl could see was the reflection of the full-shine moon trembling on the water's surface.

Nyroc flew without direction away from the pond. Who am I

now, without a home, without even the scroom of a father? And with a mother from whom I must flee? What is to become of me? Where shall I go? Where shall I find happiness? Perhaps happiness is too much to ask for. Peace. Yes, peace will do.

CHAPTER ONE

Outcast Without a Name

But this was not to be, Nyroc realized as he flew into the night. Neither peace nor happiness would be his yet. He was supposed to do something first. He just couldn't remember quite what. Since he had fled the Pure Ones, so much had happened. These last few days seemed like a tangled dream in Nyroc's brain. First, there had been the fire in Silverveil. It had been terrible and yet beautiful. And something very dangerous had happened. Nyroc, who could read fire, had become transfixed — fire-dazed. He could not move to escape the heat and flames that were pressing closer and closer to him. Finally, he had broken free. It had been a name from some half-forgotten dream that had jolted him from the grip of flames just in the nick of time. The name was "Otulissa" and though he had no idea who this Otulissa was, he felt, for some reason, that she was a Spotted Owl.

He had flown from those flames as hard and as fast as he could and soon found himself being guided by a good scroom toward a strange ghostly forest. He hadn't known that there were such things as good scrooms, but he immediately sensed that this one was good. She, too, was a Spotted Owl, but quite elderly, not the one he had dreamed about. They had settled on one of the silvery branches of the white-barked trees that grew thickly on a peninsula that jutted out into the Sea of Hoolemere. It was the closest he had ever been to this sea and he remembered longing desperately to fly across it to the Great Ga'Hoole Tree. But no, he couldn't, he recalled. The scroom had said he must do something first, that there was some task to complete, or journey to make, but before she could tell him exactly what it was, she had dissolved into the morning mist.

So where was he now? He looked over his starboard wing to the forest below. It was not as beautiful as Silverveil, but still a lovely forest. Thick green moss, a mixture of hardwood and softwood trees. Plenty of hollows! Nyroc was done with stumps, with holes in the ground, with crannies in cliffs like the one he had shared with his mother. No, he wanted to live in a nice hollow, high up in a sturdy tree where he could hear the wind in the branches, see the sky. He would fit it out with rabbit-ear moss if he could find any. Make it all cozy. And then he would hunt,

hunt like a normal owl. He would bring his prey back to the tree and eat it in the coziness of his own hollow.

He had had enough of hiding out, of always hunting in daylight, of keeping this un-owlish schedule for fear of being tracked down by Nyra or rejected outright by the nearby owls because he resembled his vicious parents.

He was bigger now, braver, smarter. He would simply explain himself, tell owl folk that he was nothing like his parents.

So, a task to complete, a journey to make, but first things first, Nyroc thought. *I must look for a hollow.*

He was half a league away now from the lake haunted by his father's scroom and he saw a nice grove of fir trees beneath him. Fir trees, he had heard, often had excellent hollows. He circled over the grove several times to look for a good tree. But just as he was about to begin his banking turn, three of the hugest owls he had ever seen swooped in on him. Nyroc felt his gizzard lurch. They were Great Grays. Every owl knew about Great Grays. They were among the biggest and most ferocious of all owls. It had been a Great Gray who had killed his father, Kludd.

"What's your name?" demanded the Great Gray on his port wing .

3

"Nyr —" But before he had even finished, the three owls were screeching at him.

"What did I tell you, Silvertip? It's him. Looks just like his mum, right down to the scar!"

Great Glaux, thought Nyroc. *Not only my scar has branded me but my name as well!*

"You're outta here, owl!" one of the Grays shrieked.

The three owls were pressing in on him, so that he could barely control the direction of his flight. "Look, I'm alone," Nyroc told them.

"You better be!" said another. "There've been rumors that your mum's fixing for another attack. Hireclaws flocking to her!"

"I'm not with her. I fled from her. I hate her!" There. He had finally said it.

They were now driving him down toward a lake and steering him to a sycamore tree. As they lighted down on a branch of the tree, the third and oldest of the three Great Grays stepped forward.

"Look, young'un, how do we know you ain't a slipgizzle for them Pure Ones?"

"A slipgizzle?" Nyroc had no idea what a slipgizzle was.

"A spy," the owl explained.

"I can't stand the Pure Ones, I tell you. I can't stand them."

"Why should we trust you?" the owl called Silvertip demanded.

"Why should we take your word?" the smallest of the Great Grays said. He was still much bigger than Nyroc.

The older one spoke again. "Perhaps, young'un, you'll prove yourself someday. But until that day, we suggest you leave. Yes, leave, or if you want . . ."

"He's got to leave Ambala, now, Tup."

"Ambala? I'm in Ambala?"

"Yes," the one called Tup said. "We are a peaceable place. We have suffered a lot through the years, first from the owls of St. Aggie's when they stole the eggs from our very nests, and then from the Pure Ones. But since the last great battle when the Guardians of Ga'Hoole defeated them, we have had peace. We don't want any more trouble."

"I promise I won't be any trouble."

"Promises aren't enough, young'un," Tup said. There was a tinge of sympathy in his voice. He looked to his companions. "But seeing as it's getting on to breaklight, why don't we let him stay another day?"

There was some grumbling from the other two.

Then Silvertip spoke. "Well, as long as he agrees to stay right in this sycamore. There's a hollow farther up the trunk that'll do for the night."

"Thank you," Nyroc said meekly. "That is very kind of you."

The third Great Gray added, "Well, you might change your mind about staying in that hollow. It's haunted, you know."

"Hortense, no need to frighten him."

"Well, I just thought he should know," Hortense said.

"What's haunted?" Nyroc asked and looked at the owl called Hortense, an odd name for a male owl, he thought.

"The hollow," Hortense replied.

"Haunted by my father's scroom?" Nyroc asked in alarm. But the scroom had appeared only over the lake. Never had his father's scroom followed him into a nesting place.

"Oh, no. It's haunted by a Fish Owl named Simon. Your father killed him many years ago," Hortense replied.

"What happened?" Nyroc asked with a sick feeling stealing over his gizzard.

"It was horrible." Tup spoke now. "You see, Simon was a pilgrim owl who had come here from the Glauxian Retreat in the Northern Kingdoms to do good, help the weak, serve the poor. Your father, Kludd, had just been in a bloody and fiery encounter with the Ga'Hoolian owls. His mask was actually melting on his face. It was Simon who rescued him and nursed him back to health."

"And he killed this Simon?"

The three Great Grays nodded.

"But why? Why would he kill an owl who helped him?"

Tup stepped forward on the branch and fastened his gleaming yellow eyes onto Nyroc's black ones. "Because he was a brutal, insane owl. Simon knew he had survived, and Kludd wanted everyone to think he was dead. It would work to his purposes." Tup paused, then added, "Of course, now he *is* dead."

"But your mother is far from dead," the owl called Silvertip said. "She is alive and well, and flying about getting hireclaws and Rogue smiths. They say she wants to have them make her fire claws."

"But Gwyndor refused," Silvertip said.

"Gwyndor! I know Gwyndor," Nyroc said. "He'll tell you that I'm not like my parents."

"Gwyndor ain't here to tell us any such thing, young'un," Tup replied. "He's gone to Beyond the Beyond."

"You might consider going to Beyond the Beyond yourself," Silvertip said in a thoughtful voice. "They don't ask questions there about who you are or where you come from. They don't care."

"It's a place for outcasts like yourself," Hortense added.

"Outcasts like myself," Nyroc whispered softly. *Is that what I am? Is that all I am ever to be? An outcast, destined to live in a desolate place full of creatures so desperate they have nowhere else to go?*

Was this to be Nyroc's great destiny? The sum, the end result, of his so-called free will? His gizzard twisted in confusion.

Without Nyroc noticing, the three Great Grays silently lofted themselves into the air and were gone.

For three dreary days, Nyroc slept in the fishy-smelling hollow that had been Simon's, and hunted in the patchy gray-violet light just before dawn, the dismal hours that owls called the "dregs of the night."

How Nyroc had hoped against hope that the journey about which the good scroom had spoken so vaguely would be to the Great Ga'Hoole Tree on the Island of Hoole in the middle of the Sea of Hoolemere. What could be farther away or more different from the great tree where the noblest owls on Earth lived than Beyond the Beyond? That barren landscape with fiery mountains and enormous four-legged animals running in packs, that place of desperate creatures, the outcasts of a civilized world?

Nyroc felt as if he had been chasing his own tail feathers around in an endless argument. He finally rushed out of the hollow and swooped down by the lake's edge. He tipped his face toward its shining surface just as the sun was beginning to rise, turning the dark waters a pale rose color. He stared at his reflection. He did look like his mother! *Am I not so much more than feathers and bones, talons and wings? But what?* An answer began to come to him: *I am of the same blood as my parents but not of the same gizzard, brain, or heart. The egg that held me came from the body of my mother, but I am not my mother's son, nor my father's. I am more. I know that with all my heart and with all my gizzard. I reject all that they were. I have no parents. I have no home. I am what I am but I shall never call myself Nyroc again. I have no name.*

CHAPTER TWO

Venomous Visitors

Nyroc had the eerie sensation of someone watching him, following him perhaps. He now realized he had felt this since first arriving at the sycamore tree. And when he had been by the lakeside, almost swallowed by despair, in the back of his tattered gizzard he had sensed this presence watching. But he had been too distraught to care.

Now, as Nyroc approached the sycamore, he noticed a curious green glow emanating from the hollow. Cautiously, he poked his head in, then gasped in disbelief. Two luminous, bright green snakes were suspended by their tails from a ridge in the hollow. *Nest-maids?* No, these are not the nest-maid snakes he'd heard civilized owls often had. *They can't be.*

The snakes' eyes glittered turquoise. Their fangs were long. *Nest-maids would never have such fangs!* Nyroc thought. Their tongues flicked about as if tasting the air, and they were the strangest tongues imaginable. They were forked like most snakes' tongues, but one side was pale ivory and the other was crimson. It suddenly dawned on Nyroc! He knew what kind of snakes these were. His mother had spoken of them. He had heard her talking about them to her top lieutenant, Stryker. She had wanted to recruit these snakes for a special elite unit in the Pure Ones. These were the flying snakes of Ambala. The most venomous snakes in the world!

"She sent you, didn't she?" Nyroc asked.

"Yesssssss," one hissed.

"I knew she would find me one way or the other," Nyroc whispered. "Here." He stepped into the hollow and thrust his chest out. "Just do it now. Do it quickly."

"Do what now?" the other one said. The words seemed to slither off the snake's tongue.

"Just kill me, quickly. Here, right to the heart." He nodded his head and with his beak poked the feathers on his chest.

"What isssss he talking about?" said the first snake to his companion.

"We didn't come here to kill you," said the other snake.

"But I'm not going back with you. I will never go back to her, to the Pure Ones."

There was a flash as both snakes, in one quick green fluid motion, slipped from their perches to the floor of the hollow where they arranged themselves into neat

11

coils. With their heads waving hypnotically they spoke in unison:

"We are not emisssssssssaries from the Pure Ones. We detesssst the Pure Ones."

"You do?" Nyroc blinked in amazement.

"We do," answered the first snake. "My name is Slynella and this is my mate, Stingyll."

"But you said that she sent for me?"

Both snakes nodded, looping their heads into figure eights and then resting them in a knot on top of their coiled bodies. It was rather dizzying to watch.

"So who is 'she'?" Nyroc asked.

"She is Misssssst," Slynella replied.

"She is the watcher in the woods," said Stingyll. "She has been watching you ssssince you arrived in Ambala."

"She has?"

Both snakes once more went through the elaborate nodding procedure, unknotting their heads from the figure eights and then knotting them again.

"But who is she? Why does she care about me?" Nyroc asked.

"She is a very sssssssspecial owl."

"Oh, she is an owl?"

"Mosssst definitely," Stingyll answered.

"She often ssssends us on misssssions. The lassst time, I came to save a Barn Owl by the name of Sssssssssoren."

"Soren!" Nyroc couldn't believe his ear slits. "You helped save Soren?"

"Yesssss, that was some years back. He had been badly wounded. His wound became 'gamby,' as we ssssay. My venom ssssaved him."

"Your venom saved him? I thought your venom killed."

"It does that, too." And both snakes now laughed, making a strange, slurred hissing sound.

"So who exactly is this Mist?"

"You shall sssssee. She lives with the eagles. Sssssome call her Hortenssssse."

"Wait a minute! Wait just one little minute. I have already met one Hortense, that Great Gray, very young and very rude. I didn't like him a bit."

"There are many named Hortenssssse in the foresssst of Ambala. It is an honor to be named Hortenssssse, no matter if you are born female or male. But Missst is the original Hortensssse, a hero beyond compare. They ssssay a hero is known by only one name in Ambala — Hortenssssse. But there is truly only one Hortenssssse, and she now calls herself Missssst and she lives apart from the other owls. She lives with the eagles."

"With eagles?"

Once more they nodded, but Slynella and Stingyll must have gotten tired, for this time they did only half a figure eight.

"And she really wants to meet me?"

"She does. She does, indeed."

"Does she know who I am?"

But by this time the snakes were slithering out of the hollow and casting themselves onto the breeze that stirred with the new day. Nyroc hesitated not out of fear, but astonishment. *Flying snakes! Incredible. But I am seeing them,* he thought.

"Follow usssss," Stingyll said, twisting his head around. "Follow usss!" Both snakes flattened themselves into ribbons that rippled in slow, undulating motions over the waves and billows of windy air.

Higher and higher they flew until they were far above the forest. Soon Nyroc spied a rocky promontory. Scraped by wind and scoured by endless winter storms, the rock had been worn to a smooth finish, and atop the promontory was the most enormous nest Nyroc had ever seen. Its circumference was at least the size of the crown of a very large tree. He had heard about eagles' nests but he had never seen one. No mere twigs were used in its construction. The nest was built from long, sturdy branches woven together in a seemingly haphazard fashion. And perched on its edge were two immense eagles. Between them was a figure that Nyroc could not quite make out. He was flying into a rising sun, which was difficult enough, and his day vision could not compare to his night vision. He was not quite sure exactly what he was seeing. But it seemed to him that a patch of speckled fog hovered between the two eagles. Or perhaps not fog, but Mist!

CHAPTER THREE
The Eagles' Nest

They had just alighted on the rim of the nest. The smaller eagle, the male, nodded at Nyroc and spoke. "Welcome to our aerie. My name is Streak and this is my mate, Zan." Zan made a series of nodding movements with her head. "I must explain," said Streak. "My dear mate, Zan, had her tongue torn out in battle with Skench and Spoorn, the old leaders of St. Aggie's. She is mute, but she can communicate with a language of gesture that Mist and I can understand."

Nyroc had not been able to take his eyes off the strange patch that hovered between the two eagles. The patch was now assuming a more definite form and appeared to be an elderly and somewhat shrunken Spotted Owl. He could resist no longer. He had to speak to this creature.

"Are you a scroom?" Nyroc asked.

There was a gentle churring, the sound owls make when they laugh. "No. I am known as Mist or Hortense, and I am alive, very much so."

"I don't mean to be rude," Nyroc said. "But why do you look the way you do?"

"Well, it's a long story but I'll try to make it brief. In Ambala, where I was hatched, the streams and brooks and lakes — even the ground itself — are rich in a magnetic material called flecks. It was both a blessing and a curse. Some owls were hatched with unusual powers because of the flecks. My father, for instance, could see through rock."

"See through rock?" Nyroc repeated.

"Yes. Quite amazing, isn't it? But sadly his own mother went yoicks, lost her wits and every gizzardly instinct she ever had."

"How awful." Nyroc could not think of anything worse than losing his gizzardly senses — except maybe losing his wings.

"For others," Mist, also known as Hortense, continued, "it disrupted their navigational abilities. But for me, I just suffered from being quite small. It took forever for my flight feathers to come in, and I was never a very strong flier."

"But were you always so . . . so . . ."

"So faded?" she said. "No, that has come on with age. My feathers whitened, and some became transparent." She paused a moment, then stuck her beak into her breast feathers and plucked one. "Here, take a look." She held out a small feather to Nyroc but he could not see it well enough to reach for it with his talon.

"By Glaux, I've never seen anything like that."

"Few have, obviously. Because I'm so transparent." She churred as did the eagle. Even Zan managed a sort of hiccuppy laugh. And the snakes, who had woven their bodies like bright green filaments through the branches of the nest, also laughed. "However," she went on, "being transparent has its advantages."

"That's how you were watching me, wasn't it? I've felt your presence since I first arrived."

Mist nodded. The air around her seemed to shimmer whenever she moved or churred.

"But now I have some questions for you. We have introduced ourselves, but you have not introduced yourself."

"I . . . I . . ." Nyroc felt his gizzard clinching. He might as well get it out. "I have no name. I have no family. I have no home."

"No . . . no . . . no . . ." Mist repeated and turned her head each time. The air once again shimmered. "How curious. Because I could have sworn — couldn't you, Streak and Zan? — that he bears a great resemblance to . . ."

Nyroc could hardly stand to hear it. He instinctively closed his ear slits. *They're going to say it! I know they're going to say it! It's the scar.*

"To Soren," Mist said.

The two syllables of the name seeped through despite his closed ear slits.

"What?" Nyroc nearly shrieked.

"Oh, definitely," Streak said.

"But look at my face."

"I am," Mist replied calmly.

"Look at my scar!"

"Oh, yes. That's plain to see," she said.

"But ... but ..." Nyroc stammered.

"You see, my dear, I look at an owl's eyes. That is where character resides. Deep within the glistening black of your eyes is a flicker of light, just as in Soren's eyes. Your father's eyes never had it. Nor do your mother's. Her eyes are as black as river stones, polished as river stones, but dead, with not a flicker of that incredible dark light of Soren's."

Nyroc's gizzard was absolutely twitching. His brain was spinning. "So ... so ... so you knew all the time who I was, and where I came from?"

"Oh yes, my dear. I did."

"Why didn't you say so?"

"I guess I wanted to hear it from you. You see, I saw you last evening by the lake when you — how should I put it? — formally renounced your birthright, your parents, your home, and finally your name. And by the way, you are right. You are more. Much more!"

The thoughts that had streamed through his mind last evening came back to him now: *I am of the same blood as my parents but not of the same gizzard, brain, or heart. The egg that held me came from the body of my mother, but I am not my mother's son, nor my father's. I am more. I know that with all my heart and with all my gizzard. I reject all that they were. I have no parents. I have no home. I am what I am but I shall never call myself Nyroc again. I have no name.*

"But how could you know all that? I didn't speak that out loud by the lake. They were just my thoughts."

"That is another odd thing that I suspect was caused by the flecks. I have discovered, but only in my old age, that I can, on some occasions, read an owl's mind. Rather like my grandfather who could see through rock, no offense intended. You hardly have rocks in your head. As I said, you are much more, much more than you ever could believe, Ny —" She started to say his name but then stopped. "By the way, you must find a new name for yourself. We must call you something."

"Yes, I suppose so . . . but are you suggesting that I stay here for a while?"

"For a while, my dear. Yes."

That is all, just a while. Will I ever have a home? Nyroc thought.

Mist knew what he was thinking but she also knew that she had been intrusive enough. There were boundaries that must be respected, the privacy of the mind and the gizzard.

"Do you think I could ever go to my uncle Soren and live with him at the Great Ga'Hoole Tree?"

"Perhaps, but not yet. Remember you said you knew in your heart that you were more than what your parents were."

Nyroc nodded.

"I agree. You are much more, my dear. And there are tasks that you must first complete."

"I have to prove myself, I know. But did Soren have to prove himself before he went to the great tree?"

"Yes, but it is hard to explain." How indeed would she explain? Gwyndor had told her, after leaving the canyonlands for the last time, that Nyroc had fire sight. And he was certain that Nyroc had seen the Ember of Hoole. If this was so, it was essential that Nyroc make the long journey to Beyond the Beyond. He must retrieve the ember, or die trying. But if he succeeded, then truly . . . oh, it was almost too wonderful to think about. For what it could mean for owlkind was huge!

"But what?" Nyroc asked.

"Yes, Soren had to prove himself, but you have much more to prove."

"It doesn't seem fair. Just because my parents were horrid tyrants. I mean, I didn't ask to be born to them."

"Life isn't always fair. But it is not a question of fairness or your parents."

Nyroc blinked. "This has to do with the . . . the . . ." Nyroc could not bring himself to say the words.

"The thing you have tried not to think about. Yes, the journey to Beyond the Beyond."

Nyroc felt his gizzard quake. Everyone he met — from the scroom in the spirit wood to the Great Gray Owls and now Mist — kept telling him in one way or another that he had to go there.

"It's a place for outcasts," Nyroc said. "That's why I must go there, isn't it? It's the only place for an owl like me."

"No! Not at all!" Mist spoke severely and the air around her began to scintillate and glimmer. The sun flashed through her transparent feathers. "You must never think that. And secondly, there is no 'must' to it."

"What do you mean?"

"You have free will, my dear. The only thing you *must* do is choose: either to go there or not to go there."

"And if I choose to go there, then what?"

"You will discover what might be your extraordinary destiny."

"I don't know what to do."

"That is why you should stay here for a while. You need time to think."

"Yes, yes, I do."

"Now, about your name."

"Yes?"

"That is yours to choose, too. Do you know how to read at all?" Nyroc shook his head. "Do you know any letters?"

"Two," Nyroc replied.

"Two? Which two?"

"P and H."

Mist was slightly perplexed. These weren't letters that occurred in this young owl's name.

"Why, may I ask, P and H?"

"They were letters in the name of my best friend, Phillip. He was going to teach me all the letters and how to read, but we only got to these two . . ." Nyroc gulped, "before my mother killed him." He had tried not to think about Phillip and the horror of that day, his mother's beak ripping the Sooty Owl's heart from his chest.

Mist, too, could see that bloody day in Nyroc's mind. What a despicable creature Nyra was! The young'un needed to stay here for a while. He must be nurtured with love and stories of noble owls. Yes, she would tell him about the great tree and about the owls who, every night with sublime hearts and valiant gizzards, rose in the blackness to perform noble deeds; the owls of Ga'Hoole who spoke no words but true ones, whose only purpose was to right all wrongs, to make strong the weak, mend the broken, and make powerless those who abused the frail.

Furthermore, Mist would tell Nyroc how Soren and Gylfie had successfully resisted moon blinking with whispered recitations of the legends of Ga'Hoole, how every time they recited or even thought about these legends their brains would clear and they once more felt their gizzards begin to quicken.

That is what Mist would do. She would feed him with legends of Ga'Hoole. The young owl would be safe here in the eagles' nest. There were many rumors of Nyra and the Pure Ones regrouping, finding hireclaws and Rogue smiths. But no one would know that Nyroc was here with them, for few dared to come to the aerie with its two huge eagles and venomous flying snakes.

CHAPTER FOUR
Sky Writing

T hat's an S, that's easy! Come on, Slynella, give me a
harder letter," Nyroc called out to the snakes that
were flying above the nest.

This was how Nyroc had been learning his letters. The
two snakes would fly overhead and inscribe the sky with
the letters of the alphabet. Nyroc had proven himself a
quick learner.

"You want a hard one?" Slynella said.

"Yes!" Nyroc replied.

The green snake began knotting herself overhead into
a complicated design, but before she had even finished,
Nyroc called out, "B. It's a B."

"Okay, now for some words," Mist said. Stingyll slipped
in beside Slynella in flight. There was a great writhing in
the darkness of the night as the two green ribbons twined
and intertwined, lacing themselves together. The first
word was a name.

"Streak!" Nyroc shouted out.

"I think you are really ready to decide on a name," Mist said, looking up from her knitting. Knitting bored her, but she had learned from Gylfie who had learned from one of the nest-maid snakes at the great tree. She was doing it now only because she was trying to expose Nyroc to as many of the arts of the great tree as she could. She knew only a few, of course, but she had told him about the famous Madame Plonk who was said to sing like the hengleens of glaumora.

Nyroc knew that he must think of a name. It was not only that he was tired of being called "Hey You" or "My Dear" or "Little One," which was even worse. Besides, he wasn't so little anymore. He had grown a lot. But as much as he hated his own name, it had been with him for quite a while. He had no intention of keeping it, but he often wondered if somewhere in that name there was something good, or even something he might miss. It was rather like chopping off a wing or maybe a talon. It had been his for a long time now.

"My dear, I do not mean to intrude, but would it not help if perhaps just this once you might try to spell your original name?" She paused. "If only to say good-bye to it."

Nyroc blinked. *Yes, she is right, if only to say good-bye.*

Nyroc flew up and hovered near the two snakes. "All right," he said and began trying to sound out the name. "Nnnnn — N." The two snakes slid tail-first into each other and gracefully made the N. Between the two of them there was plenty of snake left for the next four letters.

"Mist," he called down, "is this one of those times where it could be an I or a Y?"

"Yes, dear, I'll help you here. It's a toughie. Go with Y."

Nyroc sounded out the rest of the letters for the snakes. Finally, it was there, with not a lot of snake left over. *Nyroc.*

He had spelled his own name, the name he had vowed never to use. He flew around the script in the sky. He liked the letters. He liked the way the R swooped and dipped. He especially loved the Y. It seemed lively and perky as if it were having a really good time being a Y. He didn't want to say good-bye to these letters forever. He flew over the name several times. Slynella and Stingyll were infinitely patient with him.

He flew upside down and backward, left to right, and right to left. *Hey, try that one again,* he thought. *That's it. I'll keep the letters but just reverse them.* "I've got it! I've got it!" Nyroc cried.

"My name is Coryn!"

And in that instant the two snakes reversed themselves. There was a brief tangle of green ribbon in the sky and then out of the darkness in the most beautiful script imaginable blazed the name:

CORYN

CHAPTER FIVE

A Decision Is Made

Coryn would always look upon the night of his naming as one of the happiest nights of his life. He had certainly never been happy for as long as the time he had spent with the snakes, the eagles, and Mist. He had been in the aerie for almost thirty nights. He had come at the time of full shine, passed through the dwenking of the moon until it was just a thread, a whisper of light in the sky, and watched as it had grown fatter through the newing, and now it was almost full shine again. Summer had almost ended and autumn would soon be upon them. The time of the Copper-Rose Rain, as he now knew the Guardians of Ga'Hoole called this time of year.

In these thirty nights, he had learned so much about the tree and the Guardians and the legends — although, for some reason, Mist was rather sketchy on the details of the Fire Cycle, which he was anxious to hear. But he could not fault Mist. She had taught him so much.

And it was odd but she had somehow become less

transparent to him. Perhaps it was just his imagination that filled in the vaporous form with color and shape. He could see her eyes now. They were a lovely tawny yellow. And if he looked deeper he could see the question in her eyes: *What would Coryn choose?* Yes, the time had come for him to make a decision. He must go to Beyond the Beyond or elsewhere. He could not live here in this nest forever. There was meaning to his life and he must go out into the world to find it. He was glad for his new name but, in truth, it was not the name that had made him feel different and new; it was what he had learned. He had learned to read and to write like the owls of the great tree. He had learned about the constellations in the sky and how to use them to navigate. And he had learned of his parents' bloody history. All of this made him a very different owl.

Still he knew that he would be treated as an outcast wherever he went. A new name did not change how he looked. He would be considered indistinguishable from his treacherous parents and their violent history. And it was knowing this that helped him with his decision. He must make his own history if any owl on Earth were ever to distinguish him from Nyra and Kludd and the Pure Ones.

"It's time, isn't it?" Coryn asked, looking deep into Mist's eyes. "You probably already know my decision, don't you?"

"No, actually, I do not," Mist replied. Zan and Streak pressed closer. Slynella and Stingyll draped themselves over a limb.

"How come?" Coryn was surprised.

"I willed myself not to read what you were thinking. It was hard but I just exited your mind. I didn't want to influence you."

"But you did," Coryn replied.

"Oh, dear. How?"

"By everything you taught me. I know I must go to Beyond the Beyond. I am not sure what awaits me there. I am afraid."

"Only fools pretend not to be afraid."

"But stronger than my fear is my longing to go to the great tree, to meet my uncle Soren and aunt Eglantine, to find the good part of my family. I know before I go there, I must do this. I must go to Beyond the Beyond."

"And you have chosen to do this of your own free will?" Mist asked.

"Yes, of my own free will."

And so it was planned that Coryn would leave the next night.

"I must tell you one more time, Coryn, of the rumors."

"Yes, Mist, I know." She had told him that Zan and

31

Streak had reported rumors and sightings of the Pure Ones gathering new troops and capturing young, defenseless owls.

"They've even gone in for egg stealing like St. Aggie's did years ago in Ambala," Streak said. "But this time it seems to be up in the borderlands between the Shadow Forest and Silverveil."

"Yes, of course, they have the old eggorium at St. Aggie's there in the canyonlands. I suppose they could start that up again. There is yet another rumor," Mist continued, "that one of Nyra's top lieutenants has deserted her. They are out tracking him, too. You must be careful, young'un," Mist said.

"I promise I will." Coryn wondered if his mother's old lieutenant, Uglamore, was the deserter. He had had his doubts about how loyal Uglamore was to Nyra and the whole idea of the Pure Ones. It had been Uglamore who had tried to intervene and save Phillip from being killed in the ritual known as the Special Ceremony. But Uglamore was old now. Where in the world would an old broken-down lieutenant for the Pure Ones go? *Beyond the Beyond. Of course,* Coryn thought.

He left at First Black. The two eagles and Slynella and Stingyll accompanied him as far as the border of Ambala.

He had said his good-byes to Mist privately. Mist, never a strong flier, had chosen to stay behind.

"Glauxspeed!" Streak called out and Zan signaled. The two flying snakes had been joined now by two other snakes, and the four of them wrote across the silver of the full-shine moon:

Glauxspeed Coryn

And to think, Glaux is not even the spirit of their kind. How good of them to wish me well in the name of a spirit that is not theirs.

CHAPTER SIX

A Cry in the Night

Coryn set a course due west. The constellation of the Little Raccoon was just climbing out of its burrow beyond the horizon and into the sky. To keep this course, Coryn must fly two points off the first claw of the raccoon's port front paw. How glad he was to have learned navigation. The Pure Ones navigated by certain dim instincts that were not nearly as accurate as star navigation. On this course he would fly over The Barrens, skirt the edges of Silverveil, then angle his flight north by northwest and take a straight line into Beyond the Beyond. It would be a long trip. Not all the winds were favorable this time of year. He did not fly by day, for he wanted no encounters with mobbing crows. He had nearly been mobbed once when he and Phillip had fled the Pure Ones. He did not want that to happen again. He would try to avoid owls altogether since there had been sightings of Pure Ones in some places and rumors abounding in others. He knew that at all costs he must avoid them and, as for other owls, he knew they would still treat him as an outcast.

His new name had not really changed him, either inside or out. He knew he still must prove himself as Coryn. And perhaps part of that proving was to endure — for a time — being an outcast. He could not yet even hope to go to the Great Ga'Hoole Tree. But there was no denying that he desperately wanted to go there. He wanted to hear the great harp, the strings through which the blind nest-maid snakes wove themselves to make the music that the famous old Snowy, Madame Plonk, sang. He wanted to see the parliament where the most noble owls on Earth met. He wanted to see the magnificent great hollow where the owls feasted and danced. And most of all, he wanted to fly through the great library and read the wonderful books. Coryn thought about this as he flew. In his gizzard he knew that he had made the right decision but, in truth, he was flying away from all he yearned for.

He had been traveling now for four nights, and the first sliver of the full-shine moon had been shaved off as the dwenking began. Slimmer and slimmer it would grow, and if these northerly winds strengthened by the time he reached Beyond the Beyond, it would most likely be no thicker than the thinnest filament of a down feather. But right now he was approaching the far edge of The Barrens and would soon be crossing the border into Silverveil.

He looked down. The territory was familiar. When he had first fled from his mother he had flown over just this same corner. It was in the very spot now beneath him that he had been mistaken for his mother, Nyra, by a young Burrowing Owl. It was the first time he truly realized that he had been branded by the scar and the meaning it would have for him. The young Burrowing Owl had screeched in terror when she saw him. Her mother had come out and begun screeching as well. The two owls were hysterical with fear. It had been useless to explain to them that he was not Nyra. But now as he flew over he could hear, like an echo from that night months ago, owl voices filled with fear and panic.

"You say it's gone? Was it Nyra?" A searing cry came from the burrow.

"But how could it be?"

"It wasn't Nyra. It was a male. But Mum, it was so scary! The owl said he would kill me!"

"Kill you! Great Glaux, what has this world come to?"

Coryn realized that what he thought was an echo of his past encounter was no such thing. This conversation was happening now, underground in the depths of the Burrowing Owls' burrow! Because of his acute hearing, Coryn was able to pick up much of the conversation. He cocked his head one way and then another in the same manner as when he was stalking very small prey. Something terrible had happened to the family and he knew it was the same family because right now the mother was crying, "Harry! Harry! What shall we do?"

Harry had been the name he had heard the mother call before when she had first seen Coryn. Harry was her mate. But what was happening now? Shrieks and lamentations seemed to spill from the hole of the burrow. They were underground. They would not see him. So he decided to continue flying in tighter circles over the burrow. He scanned for a variety of sounds and honed in precisely on the source. Contracting the muscles of his facial disk, the words began to pour into his ear slits clearly, succinctly.

This family was in trouble. An egg that was very close to hatching had been stolen by a Pure One. *So* they *were here!* Coryn listened more closely. He wanted to find out the identity of the owl who had done this.

"It's not your fault, Kalo," the father was saying in a soothing voice. "There's no way you could have fought them off."

Them? More than one? Who was it? Had Nyra gotten hireclaws?

"We're not the first family to be attacked," the mother was sobbing. "It's happening all over Silverveil. But I never thought they'd come this far into The Barrens. I mean, our burrows are hard to find."

"They probably have slipgizzles," said another voice.

"No, they probably followed us here from Silverveil. Harry, it's all your fault. I knew we shouldn't have spent the summer in that stupid tree in Silverveil. Burrowing Owls do not belong in forest trees. They belong in burrows in barren lands like this or in deserts." She began to wail again.

This was exactly the same argument Coryn had heard them having a few months before. The father had wanted to spend the summer in Silverveil. The mother had not, and now she was blaming the father for the stolen egg. Coryn's gizzard trembled in sympathy, and his heart went out to the family even though they had screeched the most horrible imprecations and insults at him when they had thought he was Nyra. But what was to be done? He had better get out of here right away before they all stormed out of the burrow ready to wreak vengeance on the first Pure One they saw — for which he would undoubtedly be mistaken.

But wait! Coryn thought. Perhaps there was a way he could help them. Maybe he could find that egg. If the rumors of Pure Ones' activities in Silverveil were true and if they had been followed, as the female Burrowing Owl had claimed, maybe he could try to retrace their flight path. Instinct told him that the Pure Ones would not be flying these eggs back to the canyonlands one at a time. Since there had been so many tales of them in and around Silverveil, this might be where they had temporarily taken the eggs. Furthermore, since the female Burrowing Owl had been so reluctant to spend the summer in Silverveil, the family most likely had gone to a part of the forest that was closest to The Barrens. This might not be far off his course to Beyond the Beyond. It would certainly be worth it if he could retrieve their stolen egg.

CHAPTER SEVEN

A Heartbeat Calls

The border between The Barrens and Silverveil was a long one, stretching from the Shadow Forest to the west, all the way to the Sea of Hoolemere in the east. As Coryn flew, he gave further thought to the Pure Ones' strategy for snatching eggs. If Nyra was anything, she was practical. She would have her lieutenants set up a cache for the stolen eggs. Then she would borrow or steal a coal bucket from a Rogue smith for transport so that several eggs might be taken at once.

By Coryn's reckoning, the egg cache would be limited to a triangle at the juncture of Silverveil and the Shadow Forest, right at the northern corner of The Barrens. He would have to be careful. He was wondering if he should return to his old ways of flying in daylight rather than night. In daylight, he would risk mobbings by crows. At night, he would risk encounters with the Pure Ones. *Some choice!*

He flipped his head straight up as he flew, then rotated it in the widest arc possible. Clouds were coming in. Low woolly ones. And the moon, being just a sliver, was not bright. He could fly above or even within the clouds. They would camouflage him perfectly and every now and then he could poke his head out to survey the territory. He had flown this country before, and he realized that he had very good instincts for memorizing flight routes and land. No matter what the weather might be, each territory generated its own peculiar wind currents. Not only that, the sounds were different depending on whether they came from the hardscrabble part of The Barrens or the vast prairies, which were covered in grass that made the wind sing. It was the same with the forests. Each forest had its distinct sounds.

And perhaps most important of all, he was very familiar with the flight sounds of the Pure Ones. They flew fast and they flew noisily. Their plummels, those soft fringe feathers that edged the wings of most owls, were stiff and ratty from lack of care. He had learned from Mist how to take proper care of his plummels, and he remembered swelling with pride when she had told him that he finally was flying as quietly as a Guardian of Ga'Hoole.

So Coryn began to spiral upward and penetrate the low, scudding clouds. But he had forgotten one thing. Clouds were wet. He plumped up his feathers to disperse the fine droplets. It wasn't a downpour but he had to give a bit of a shake every once in a while to shed the moisture that was building up.

He hadn't been flying long when he sensed a distinct change in the landscape beneath him. Sounds softened. He knew he was over the lush green valleys and thick stands of trees of Silverveil. The silence would grow even denser the closer he got to the Shadow Forest, where evergreens covered most of the land, climbing up the steepest hills of the deepest valleys. And the wind would have a different sound when blowing through the needles rather than ruffling through leaves or the bare branches of deciduous trees. He once again cocked his head, but this time he was not after prey. He was listening for predators, predators most vile, most despicable, predators who preyed on the unhatched young of decent families like the Burrowing Owls of The Barrens.

He began to hear something. Voices whispering directly below him. The words were almost indistinguishable, but he thought he heard another sound running beneath the words. An odd sound that he had never in his life heard before — almost as if something were swishing, but it was not a pond. He had roosted in stump hollows by ponds before. He knew the sound their waves made lapping the shore when the wind rippled the surface. This was not the same at all. This was a muffled rushing noise — like a river? No. Like an ocean? *But I have never heard the sounds of an ocean. I have never been that close to Hoolemere.* Besides, oceans were vast and this sound was small. Very small, like a tiny ocean in ... *an egg!* The realization seemed to burst in his brain and sent a sizzle through his gizzard. And within the depths of that miniature ocean, he heard something else. A heartbeat!

He drifted out of the clouds, scanning the sky below and the forest for any sign of the Pure Ones. He was a good half league from the source of the sound he had identified as that of not just one egg but several. He realized now that even if he did get to the eggs, he could rescue only one and it had to be that of the Burrowing Owl. How would he know which one was the Burrowing Owl's egg? He'd never seen any owls' eggs in his entire life.

Well, first things first, Coryn thought again. He had to get closer to the source. One thing gave his gizzard a boost: He had not recognized any of the voices he had heard guarding the cache of eggs. That meant his mother was not there. Nor was Stryker, her fiercest lieutenant. In fact, the voices sounded rather young. Not much older than himself. Probably the rumored new recruits, so perhaps they might not recognize him. Oh, but of course they would! He looked so much like Nyra and then there was the cursed scar. How could he have forgotten? Even if they had never seen him, they had probably heard about . . .

Coryn stopped. A realization seized him mid-flight and sent a jolt to the deepest part of his gizzard. He lighted on the branch of the tree directly beneath him, a creaking old oak draped in thick moss. Small bits and pieces, mere fragments of ideas, began to link together in his mind. Perhaps for once his resemblance to his mother, scar and all, could work in his favor.

Coryn's brain worked faster. He could do this, he knew it. He stared hard at the scrim of moss hanging from the limb in front of the one where he was perched. It reminded him of something. Yes, of course, those hagsfiends that had swooped down on him when he had first fled from The Barrens the last time. They looked like tattered owls, shrouded in shreds of gray mist. They were hagsfiends, the hellish witches from the owl hell known as hagsmire. His mother had told him frightening stories of these fiends, and now this moss reminded him of them.

He looked up at the moss scarves waving eerily in the breeze. Reaching up, he pulled down a long piece of it. It fell perfectly over his shoulders, trailing off the edges of his wings. He flipped his head around and nipped up one edge with his beak so that it fell like a hood over the top of his head. He didn't want to hide his face completely. The scar should show. Coryn then spread his wings and lifted off from the branch where he had perched.

The raccoon, ground squirrel, mouse, rat, and lynx paused in their nightly bustle as they foraged for food and looked up at the strange creature that flew overhead. A tree squirrel that had just poked its nose out to go on its evening rounds for nut collecting backed quickly into its knothole. A skunk sprayed its noxious odor into the sky, but to no avail. Coryn was much too high in flight. A deathly quiet fell upon the forest. A hagsfiend was abroad!

CHAPTER EIGHT

A Fiend Comes to Life

"Why's everything suddenly so quiet?" the young Barn Owl asked.

"I don't know. It's weird, isn't it?" replied the other.

"Yeah, it gives me the creelies." "Creelies" was the owl word for deep, unidentifiable fears.

"Well, you better get over it, you two. This is our test. Going into battle is going to give you bigger creelies than this. All we have to do is guard these eggs until Stryker and Wortmore get back."

Coryn had settled into a tree downwind of the three owls guarding the eggs. He hoped the wind would carry away any sound he made and would carry to him all the words and sounds coming from the three owls guarding the egg cache. And, at this moment, he seemed to be bombarded by sounds. There were the voices of the three owls and then there were the stirrings of the eggs. These eggs sounded close to hatching. He did not think there were that many, maybe three or four. But still there was the problem of which one was the Burrowing Owls' egg. He needed to listen more closely. The more he could learn, the better off he would be. But he did not have much time if Stryker and Wortmore were expected. What he had already learned was valuable. There were three of them. They were all Barn Owls, which meant that they were in training for higher jobs and would not be assigned to the lowliest ranks of the Pure Ones like his dear friend, Phillip. And they were nervous. Even the one who sounded so bold was nervous. Coryn could tell. He could hear the young recruit's heart beating rapidly.

Coryn's hearing had never been so sharp. He could hear things he had never before heard. He continued to cock his head and scan with his ear slits for any new scrap of information. He was almost sure that there were three eggs in the cache, for he could hear the dim but slightly different heartbeats of the unhatched chicks. They were more like soft pulses than real beats. He cocked his head, and then again. Was there another pulsing sound coming from beneath the hollow that the three Barn Owls guarded? He stilled his own heart and quieted his breathing. It was as if Coryn had transmuted his entire body into one big ear. He opened his eyes wide in amazement. *There is an egg at the base of the tree. Perhaps in a shallow pit covered with something. Of course! This is the egg of a Burrowing Owl. This is where a Burrowing Owl's egg would be kept.*

"Did you hear something, Flint?"

"No. You two are just getting jumpy."

"It . . . it . . . sounded like a very soft wind."

"So, it was a soft wind. Never heard of wind in a forest?"

"I don't know. It just sounded different."

Coryn made two more passes high above the tree where the three owls were perched, guarding the eggs. He could hear their rapidly increasing heartbeats. He didn't want to wait much longer. Now was the time. He slowed his flight and spiraled down and then began to hover. It was perfect timing as the cloud cover parted and a misty trail of moonlight slipped through the trees.

"Nyra!" one of them screamed.

"Not Nyra! Her hagsfiend's come to curse you." And then Coryn let loose with a terrifying shree.

> *Your gizzards are a-wobble,*
> *Your gall grot turned to mush.*
> *I shall take you all to hagsmire*
> *And rip out all your guts.*
> *I shall make you my slaves,*

Condemn you to shame,
Unless you learn to play
My great and evil game.

"My Glaux! My Glaux! Save us!" Flint was gasping.

"We should never have left our parents!"

"It's not my fault. I was snatched!"

The three Barn Owls were fleeing, spiraling upward in flight. They could not leave their post quickly enough. It had worked!

CHAPTER NINE

The Egg Restored

Coryn tore off the scarves of moss. The great ruse had worked better than he had ever dreamed. He lighted down at the base of the tree and carefully cleared away the leaves from the shallow pit. There was the egg, perfectly round and gleaming white, with still a little bit of dirt from The Barrens stuck to its shell.

Ever so cautiously, Coryn wrapped his talons around the precious egg. Then he spread his wings and, with a powerful upstroke followed by a downstroke, lifted off the ground. He felt bad that he could not save the other three in the nest, yet he would not even have known where to take them. All he knew right now was that he had to get out of this forest before Stryker and Wortmore came back. The wind had shifted and was against him. It would be a hard flight back to The Barrens but he had to do it. There was little left of the night. He might have to risk flying into the morning, but there was really no choice.

The cloud cover had blown off. There was no place to

hide now in the sky. He could only hope that he would not meet any of the Pure Ones. Perhaps he should have kept the rags of moss. It had certainly worked as a hagsfiend disguise. But flying against this wind with the moss would not have been easy. He could feel now the swish of the liquid in the egg and hear the murmurs of the young heart. How precious these feelings and sounds were. How precious this life was. To think that it could have been destroyed by the Pure Ones. Surely, it would have been as good as destroyed even if it had hatched, because to be born into such a despicable world and nurtured by such vile creatures was the same as death.

He pumped his wings harder against the wind. It was amazing how quickly he had come to love this egg and, with that wonder, Coryn realized something else: To love something can often mean to give it up, to release it to where it truly belongs. Was life always going to be this way for him? Coryn wondered. He had loved Phillip and he had loved Mist and Zan and Streak and the lovely green snakes and yet he was forced to part with them all.

The sky was beginning to lighten. He could see the mound of rocks beneath which the Burrowing Owls had dug their burrow. There was nobody out of the burrow at this hour. They were probably sleeping below. He was not quite sure how he should go about giving them back the egg. He didn't want to scare them again. But he certainly couldn't just leave the egg outside to be found. The wrong owls might find it. Not to mention snakes, which loved to eat any kind of bird's eggs.

As Coryn began to descend, he heard a soft weeping sound coming from the burrow. It was the mother. Then there were the murmurs of the father trying his best to soothe her.

Now how should I do this? Coryn thought. He lighted down and gently placed the egg just to the side of the entrance. The sunrise behind the egg was creeping over the dawn horizon, making the egg cast a lovely cool shadow over the entrance to the burrow. Below in the burrow, Harry blinked as he patted his wife and looked up, noticing this change in the light.

"Just a minute, dear, I want to check something outside."

Coryn turned away from the burrow's entrance. He could not face this owl. His gizzard was shivering so hard it seemed to shake his entire body. He heard a gasp.

"What? What is this? Myrtle, come here. It's a miracle. Our egg, our egg is back!"

There was a racket as the rest of the family clambered from the burrow.

"How? How did this happen?" Myrtle asked.

It was a minute before anyone noticed Coryn off to the side, almost hiding himself behind a rock with his face still turned away.

"This was no a miracle." It was a young female owl who spoke. Coryn could hear the scratches of her talons against the hard gritty earth and rock as she came toward him. "You . . ." She hesitated. "You brought our egg back, didn't you?"

Coryn nodded but still would not turn around. He could hear the rapid heartbeat of the young owl. She was coming closer. He buried his head beneath one wing.

"Won't you turn around so we can see you?" she said softly. "Please!"

Slowly, Coryn began to turn around, but his wing was still lifted against his face.

"Who are you?" Myrtle asked.

"Why are you hiding your face?" asked the young daughter.

"Because," Coryn began slowly, "I am not who you think I am. As I told you before, I am nothing like my mother or father. My name is not Nyra, I am Coryn." And he let his wing drop from his face.

There was a gasp and a little shriek from the young

daughter, Kalo. But then she stepped forward. She extended her wing and touched Coryn gently. "We believe you. You brought our egg back. We believe you."

"Please come into our burrow," Harry said. "Please, son, come in."

He called me son. No one has ever called me son.

CHAPTER TEN
A Namesake

The little egg deep in the burrow began to rock slightly.

"Watch it carefully now, Coryn. It will sort of shudder," Kalo whispered.

"Shudder?" Coryn asked.

"Yes. All eggs do just before they hatch. I really shuddered. Mom said I was the biggest egg she ever laid," Kalo offered.

"Hush up," said Myrtle. "This isn't a contest. It's a hatching, a birth!"

And it's a miracle, Coryn thought.

A miracle and a dream. It had been only two nights since he had arrived at the burrow but he felt as if he had entered a dream. A dream family. There was a young owl his age, a mum and da who loved and nurtured her. There was gentle bickering between the parents, and some squabbling and teasing. But there was love. And now for the first time ever, he was seeing a chick hatch.

"Look, Myrtle, there's the egg tooth coming through."

"Egg tooth?" Coryn wondered aloud.

"Didn't your mum tell you about the egg tooth?" Kalo said with a small giggle.

"My mum told me nothing," Coryn sighed. *Nothing except false stories of glory, conduct of so-called valor that were really deeds of shame, tales of so-called honor that were in truth histories of disgrace, codes of loyalty that were in fact schemes of hatred and vengeance. Yes, that is what Nyra taught me.*

"The egg tooth, my dear," Myrtle began, "is a tiny sharp tooth that has only one purpose: to help a chick peck its way out of the shell. It disappears soon after hatching."

They all watched spellbound now as a long crack began crinkling out from the tiny hole.

"The 'Fracture of Glaux' some call it," Harry whispered.

"Get ready!" Kalo said. "It's coming! I bet it's a ..." She started to say she thought it would be a boy, but Harry cuffed her wings gently. "What did I tell you? We don't bet on such things. We just thank Glaux that we have our precious egg back."

There was a loud crack now as the egg split open. A shiny blob of a chick flopped out. Coryn was shocked. It was one of the most disgusting things he had ever seen — featherless, slimy with bulging eyes, *but ... but ... I love it!* Never had he felt such a swirl of emotions. It was ugly yet adorable. It was repulsive yet lovable. It was gooey with slime but he wanted to cuddle it. He watched transfixed as the tiny thing attempted to stagger to its feet and then collapsed.

"It's a boy!" Myrtle cooed. Then she looked up. "And we'll call him Coryn!"

"What?" Coryn said.

"Of course, Coryn!" Harry repeated. Then hoorays broke out in the burrow.

"I . . . I don't know what to say."

"You don't have to say anything," Kalo spoke softly. "If it hadn't been for you . . ."

"Yes, Coryn. If it hadn't been for you . . ." Myrtle's eyes filled with tears.

And then began all the wonderful little ceremonies that mark an owl's life soon after hatching. The "Firsts" they were called. Coryn felt the most touching of all these ceremonies was the First Seeing ceremony, when the little chick first opened its bulging eyes and took a peek at its new world.

"Just think," Kalo whispered as little Coryn looked about. "He thinks this burrow is the whole world and there are only five owls in it!" That ceremony was followed usually by the First Worm or Insect ceremony, and Coryn was allowed to bring him his very first worm. Then there was the First Down ceremony when the first fluffy filaments of downy feathers began to sprout from the naked chick's puckery skin.

"Oh, you'll be a regular little fluff-ball soon," Harry said as he fussed over his son. "Here, chickie-chickie poo-poo!"

"Da's absolutely besotted!" Kalo said.

"Besotted?" Coryn asked.

"Fancy word for being in love, like yoicks with love," Myrtle said. "Kalo is always using fancy words. 'Besotted' is her latest one."

But it was perfect, Coryn thought. He, too, was besotted. It sounded to him like being soggy with love — not simply yoicks or crazy.

It would be so hard to leave. He felt as if he could stay in this burrow forever. He had already stayed too long, nearly five nights. They were now begging him to stay for little Coryn's First Meat ceremony, which would be in another two nights. But he knew he couldn't. This would be his last night. He would have to leave by First Black the next evening. But for tonight he and Kalo — with whom he had grown very close — would go out and hunt for that first meat together.

Night flying with Kalo was very interesting. Kalo spent almost as much time on the ground poking into rats' nests and molehills as she did in the sky. Coryn supposed that this was the way it was with most Burrowing Owls, because they were known for their excellent walking skills and their long, strong, featherless legs.

He was perched on a rock with a dead mouse firmly beneath one talon. It was curious, he thought. At first, he found the featherless legs of Burrowing Owls unattractive, almost disgusting. But now as he watched Kalo striding toward a molehill, he thought them downright pretty. And she looked so elegant as she walked. Her tail didn't drag at all on the ground like most owl tails would have. And just the way her shoulders set was something special. It wasn't, however, simply how Kalo looked. She was smart. *Oh, why, oh, why do I have to leave everything nice behind and go beyond? To Beyond the Beyond!*

Kalo came back as Coryn was in the midst of all these thoughts.

"It's grosnik," she said as she lofted herself onto the rock beside him.

"Grosnik? What's that?"

"You've never heard of grosnik?" She blinked.

"No."

"Well, there were only baby moles in the nest. We don't eat baby anything. We call it grosnik."

"Oh, you're talking about standards!" Coryn replied.

"Yes, standards. But 'grosnik' is the word used for forbidden food — at least among Burrowing Owls."

"My best friend, Phillip, told me about such standards. You see, his father once had to kill a baby fox when they were starving to death."

"Oh," Kalo said and was very quiet for a moment. Coryn hoped that she didn't think poorly of him because he had had a friend whose father killed a baby. "Coryn, I know so little about you, really, except where you came from and who your parents were."

"Isn't that enough?" Coryn looked down at the dead mouse clamped beneath the toes of his talons.

"Not really. I don't mean to pry. But this is the first time you have ever mentioned a best friend. And why must you leave us tomorrow? Why must you go to Beyond the Beyond?"

Coryn sighed. "I am not even exactly sure myself, Kalo." He didn't want to tell her about his fire sight. It was such a freakish thing. He didn't want to scare her in any way. "You know sometimes that you just have to do something. You might not be sure why."

"Like you had to bring the egg back to us."

"Well, yes, but I knew that was the right thing to do. It was simple."

"Simple! Are you yoicks? There was nothing simple

about it, Coryn. You were incredibly courageous." Coryn felt a delicious quivering in his gizzard. "You must know that this is the right thing to do."

"Yes, yes. That's it," Coryn said. "I wouldn't dare do it if I thought it was wrong. If I thought it was grosnik."

Kalo churred softly.

"Why are you laughing?"

"It's just that grosnik is usually a word meant for food, forbidden food, but I know what you mean. You wouldn't do it if you thought it was against your standards."

"Yes, that's it," said Coryn.

"But, Coryn, would you tell me about your friend, Phillip?"

"It's a very sad story. Are you sure you want to hear it?"

"Yes, Coryn, I am your friend. That is what friends are for, to share the sad stories as well as the happy ones."

So Coryn told Kalo about Phillip, and together the two young owls wept in the moonlight.

CHAPTER ELEVEN
Listening to Legends

The last thing the family of Burrowing Owls told Coryn before he left the following evening was that he should be careful of the Pure Ones.

Then Harry had said, "I have heard rumors, however, that Nyra has been killed."

"What?" Coryn had said.

"Yes, her scroom, or some say it was a hagsfiend, was spotted in the southwest corner of Silverveil near the border of the Shadow Forest."

It was all Coryn was able to do to keep from bursting out laughing. He had never told the Burrowing Owls, not even Kalo, of his ruse. Apparently, it had worked better than he ever dreamed.

And, indeed, there were rumors!

The northerly winds had continued to build and it had taken several days of very slow flying to reach the edge of the Shadow Forest. He had found what he thought was only an empty hollow in a fir tree. But now as the sun rose high in the sky, he could hear the voices of a family of Great Horned Owls talking.

"They say a hagsfiend of Nyra was spotted over by Cape Glaux."

"Cape Glaux? I thought it was just in the southern part of Silverveil."

"Well, there was another rumor that her scroom was in Ambala."

"Hagsfiend, scroom — there are rumors all over the place. The important question is: Is she dead or not? Hagsfiends can't lead armies. They can just scare owls, but they have no real power."

"At least not anymore," another owl added.

The conversation was fascinating. The dry wood of the tree was a perfect conductor for the family's every word.

"What do you mean, not anymore?"

My question precisely, Coryn thought.

"In ancient times . . ."

"You mean the time of the legends, Da?"

Coryn's gizzard quickened. Nothing stirred him like hearing the fragments of the legends of Ga'Hoole. When he had first fled from the Pure Ones and spent the long winter hiding out in tree stumps, flying by day and sleeping by night, his only solace had been to listen to the bedtime stories and legends told by parents to their young'uns toward dawn. He had heard mostly fragments, rarely complete stories. Now he pressed his ear slit to the rough wood of the hollow's sides.

"In the time of the Coming of Hoole, when Grank, the first collier, rescued the egg that was the good King Hoole."

Rescued the egg! The egg of good King Hoole! Coryn's gizzard did a flip-flop, his heart skipped a beat.

"The hagsfiends tried to snatch that princely egg. But Grank saved it and even raised it in the great Northern Kingdoms in a secret forest far from any other owls. But when Hoole was no longer a hatchling, somehow the hagsfiends and other evil owls found out where he was, and Grank and Hoole were forced to flee to Beyond the Beyond. Some say it was Grank's plan all along to take the young prince there, for that was where his education would be completed. You know that Grank was not only the first collier, and a great one at that, but he had what some called wizardly powers. He had fire sight."

The similarity to recent events in Coryn's life seemed both incredible and confusing. Was the egg he had rescued that of a king? Was little Coryn destined to be king and save the owl universe? Was he himself, like Grank? *No wonder I must go to Beyond the Beyond. For if I am to be little*

Coryn's teacher, maybe it is in Beyond the Beyond that I'll complete my education to become a wizardly owl. And Grank had had fire sight just like I do! Coryn had never heard this detail before. And didn't it make sense that he should become little Coryn's tutor since he had rescued the egg? Oh, there were too many coincidences to be ignored. Coryn could hardly wait to leave for Beyond the Beyond.

Now he finally knew why he must go. If he had only known this when Kalo asked him why he was going. *But then again*, he thought, *that might have been a little too much.* He tried to imagine himself saying to her, "Well, you see, Kalo, your little brother, the egg I rescued, he's actually a king and I am supposed to be his tutor. Therefore I have to go to Beyond the Beyond to complete my education before I can start helping your brother."

First Black couldn't come too soon! Coryn was very excited but finally he slept. He was awakened hours later at tween time, by the rustling in the Great Horned Owls' hollow as they prepared to go out and hunt. He would wait until they left and then he would find the Star That Never Moves in the north sky and take his bearings as Mist and the eagles had taught him. He would head four points west of the star into Beyond the Beyond. This was his destiny: to teach a prince to become a king.

CHAPTER TWELVE
Wolves in the Moonlight

As Coryn left the Shadow Forest for Beyond the Beyond, the contrary winds increased and he was forced to stop again and again. He tried flying through the trees rather than above them, thinking that this would afford him more wind protection. But the branches of the trees were being tossed wildly, and dodging them was as much of an effort as flying against the wind. Then when the winds finally died down one morning, he was tempted to fly in the light of day. Tempted, that is, until he heard the loud cawing of crows. *Why get mobbed now*, he had thought, *after all this flying*. So he counseled himself to be patient. He slept through that day, then flew night after night, stopping only to hunt enough to keep up his strength. And always, always he avoided the notice of other owls. Finally, he reached his destination.

The sky sparkled with stars. The moon was full and low, a "perching moon," owls often called it as it seemed to perch like an immense silver ball on the horizon.

The moon appeared to tremble slightly as if it might fall off the horizon. *This could be the edge of the world,* Coryn thought, for it seemed as if he had indeed flown far enough to take him to the edge of the world.

Coryn had perched on a high ledge just within the border of Beyond the Beyond and was surveying the strangest landscape he had ever seen. It was an unimaginable landscape and yet he had seen it before — in the fire that Gwyndor had made to burn the bones of Kludd, his father.

Everything about this place was strange, even its color. There were patches of snow and between these patches of white, the land glistened black for the most part. But oddest of all — and this, too, he had seen in the flames of the fires — were the weird cone-shaped mountains. On top of them were openings like huge mouths that belched steam and occasionally fire into the night. Like streaks of boiling blood, coals spilled down their slopes.

He saw Rogue colliers in the distance flying over the cone mountains, but none of them flew near the mouths. They dove for the coals most distant from the mountaintops, the ones that were cooling at the edges of the tumbling rivers of embers.

Although Coryn had arrived only a few hours before, it was not hard to see that weapons were the main business of the Beyond the Beyond. The landscape was dotted with the glowing forges of Rogue smiths. He supposed it was because so many good coals were available for building fires. The sound of hammers striking anvils rang out constantly. And when he had taken a quick flight over one patch of forges set closely together, he saw Rogue colliers and Rogue smiths haggling over the price of embers and, farther along, hireclaws and Rogue smiths arguing over the price of a set of battle claws. He hadn't seen this much activity in a long time.

Returning from this brief foray to his perch on the high ledge, something else drew his attention — a swift silken movement against the horizon. It flowed like a river but clearly was no river. And as it crossed the perching moon it darkened. Soon there were black shadows printed against the silver roundness of the moon. Coryn's gizzard quickened. He had seen these figures before. These were the weird long-legged creatures loping across the land that he had seen in Gwyndor's fire. Yes! One turned now to look at him. Even at this distance, Coryn could see the creature's eyes — two sparkling green slits!

The creatures were beautiful to watch. They seemed to flow rather than run, to stream like liquid, like a river. The line of animals gradually turned toward the ridge where Coryn perched and he saw the glint of many green eyes, the greenest green he had ever beheld. Not the soft velvety

68

green of moss, or the dark green of the fir or pine, or the blue-green of the spruce tree. No, if fire were green, this was what it would look like — sparkling, fizzing with intensity. But where were they going?

In another second it became clear. While Coryn had been concentrating on the distant view, another strange herd of animals had appeared. Larger than the River Legs, as Coryn now thought of them, and spindly but with odd, branchlike things on top of their heads. *Why would an animal wear branches on its head?* Coryn wondered.

One of the River Legs broke away from the group. It circled wide around the Running Trees that had sped up. It seemed to scan the herd and then quickly found one lagging at the rear and steered it away from the rest of the Running Trees. It bolted ahead. Another River Legs suddenly streaked up with an amazing blast of speed on the other side of the bolting animal. Then it slowed down in such a way that the Running Tree could not return to its herd.

Coryn lifted off the ledge where he perched and began to follow the pursuit. It was fascinating. The River Legs were using a very complicated strategy. He was sure that the two chasing the Running Tree were capable of greater speed, but it seemed as if they deliberately chose to keep their pace steady with their intended prey. Perhaps they were trying to tire it out so it would not fight so hard at the kill. He knew that certain birds did this. The Running Tree had now slowed considerably as it came to a patch of ground free of snow. It began to graze, casually, as if it did not have a care in the world.

Is the animal yoicks, or what? Coryn thought. He was dimly aware of another bird flying near him in the vicinity. Not an owl, but most likely a raven, from the sound of its wing beats.

Now he saw that the other River Legs had drawn closer. They sunk their bodies down close to the grass and were creeping toward the Running Tree. From his vantage point high above, Coryn could see that they were stalking the animal. The Running Tree raised its head and scanned the area. *It must be terrifically dumb, blind, or have no sense of smell,* Coryn thought as the creature went back to eating. The River Legs were stealing closer. Now Coryn observed one of the River Legs give a signal to another. It did something with its tail. The other hunter noticed it and was off. The signal seemed to spread through the River Legs. They formed a circle around the animal, tightening it every few moments through some invisible code or signal that Coryn could not understand.

The Running Tree was suddenly aware. It reared up, its eyes wild with terror. The four River Legs pounced on it and brought it down. One of the hunters slashed a hip wide open, another ripped open a shoulder. But the Running Tree staggered to its feet somehow. It stared hard at its attackers as if it were taking a death stand, as if saying, *I cannot run, but I can stand and stare you down even as you set to kill me.* Coryn was rapt. He had never seen anything like this. It was as if in that moment something was exchanged between prey and predator.

Two River Legs began to harass it by darting in quickly with bites and snaps aimed at the belly. More blood spurted out. They obviously wanted to keep the Running Tree bleeding.

The creature began to wobble on its spindly legs, and then a few seconds later, it collapsed. But Coryn could still hear its labored breathing. A single River Legs now came up. It was the animal that had originally split the Running Tree from the herd. He walked around to the head of the dying beast. Coryn flew down close. He saw the killer dip his head close to the prey. Something astonishing was happening. This was not simply a stare now. The eyes of both animals locked together. There was something ceremonial about this locking of the eyes.

Coryn knew he was right. Something was being agreed upon between the predator and the prey. It was the River Legs who now seemed submissive, as if he were asking for something, asking for the life of the Running Tree, and the Running Tree in silence was responding by saying, *I am valuable. My meat will sustain you. I am worthy.*

Then in one slash with his fangs, the River Legs opened the animal's belly and tore at its guts. There was a final gasp and then nothing.

Coryn was stunned. He had killed many animals in his young life but he had never locked eyes with them. He had never thought much about their dying. But this was a different kind of death. It seemed almost noble. There was dignity in both the killing and the dying.

He flew to a rock outcrop to watch as the rest of the River Legs came in for the feed. There seemed to be an order to this as well. Immediately after the death rip to the stomach, the River Legs threw his head back, closed his eyes, and howled. A large gray female trotted up to him. Coryn guessed that she was his mate. They ate first. Next came the other hunters, the ones that had chased the Running Tree and the ones that had brought it down and harassed it. The rest of the group next moved in, and finally the young ones — the yearlings and then the pups.

But Coryn noticed one yearling lurked around the edges seeming to beg for food. None of the others, not even the pups, would let him in for the smallest nip. His coat did not gleam like the rest; in fact, his fur was scruffy and ragged and he even had bald patches. And one of his hind legs was bent and shorter than the other. Finally, when the other River Legs moved off, he approached the remains of the carcass in a limping gait.

Coryn wondered if there might be anything left for himself. He was not even sure that he would like the taste of a Running Tree. But he was hungry. He was just about to spread his wings when a shadow passed over him.

"Not so fast, young'un. We go first."

Coryn looked up. It was the raven he had sensed earlier. There were now four others, as well. The raven lighted down on the outcropping.

"They don't call us wolf birds for nothing, you know."

"Wolf birds? I thought you were a raven."

"We are, but we follow the wolves."

"Wolves?" Coryn blinked.

"Wolves. What did you think it was that brought down that caribou? Fairy folk?"

"Fairy folk?"

The raven laughed raucously. "You're in a land of great superstition here. Before our time, the Others and such like yourself believed in little spirits with wings. They called them fairy folk."

73

"Oh." Coryn was feeling exceedingly stupid. In a moment he would feel even stupider. "I didn't know what those creatures were called. I just called them River Legs."

"River Legs! Ha!" He cawed wildly. "And what did you call the caribou?"

Coryn was almost to embarrassed to say. He sighed. "Running Trees."

With that, the raven let loose a loud and clamorous barrage of caws. "Hey, mates." He tipped his head up to the other ravens that were flying overhead.

"You know what this owl calls wolves? River Legs."

"You gotta be kidding!" one of the ravens yelled back.

"And he calls caribou Running Trees."

It felt to Coryn as if the entire sky were laughing at him now. Even the scruffy yearling wolf looked around at him.

When the raven had recovered himself, he began to speak again. "Them's not trees on its head. Them's antlers. Now, here's how it goes, laddie."

Laddie? They certainly have a strange way of speaking here, Coryn thought. It was Hoolian, but with a lot of different words and an odd accent, very similar to Gwyndor's.

"May I introduce myself first and ask your name as well?" Coryn asked.

The raven gave him a dark, piercing look. "We don't inquire about names in Beyond the Beyond. We prefer being nameless — us birds, that is. The wolves — now they're a different story. They all got names. Important to learn those. Every clan's got a name, it does. The clan that brought down that caribou, them's the MacDuncans, and Duncan be their leader."

"Clans?" Coryn asked.

"Yeah. Like family." Though not prepared to give his name, the raven seemed ready enough to talk. "Most wolves travel in packs, but these dire wolves call their packs clans. When a clan gets big, they break into two clans. So there might be as many as, say, five or six MacDuncan clans. But the main one is the one with the chieftain. And that was the main clan that took down the caribou.

"The dire wolves of these clans are bigger than any wolf you're ever going to see," the raven went on. "Special. So I guess they feel they should have a special way of naming themselves. 'Pack' just won't do. So you got your MacDuncans and your MacDuffs and your MacFangs. Oh, a whole mess of them, mostly named Mac-something."

"What about that little wolf? The one they were always chasing away."

"Oh, that fella. Hamish be his name. The ravens eat after Hamish, sometimes before he's quite finished. He doesn't seem to mind. He's a nice fella. Sad about him."

"Yes, it does seem sad. He doesn't seem exactly part of the clan. They were chasing him off. Look, all that is really left are the bones."

"Well, that's just the point, now, isn't it?" The raven blinked, cocked his head, and looked at Coryn with his beady black eyes.

"I'm afraid I don't get the point," Coryn said meekly.

"You see little Hamish there, he's got a bit of a lame leg. So he can't be a good hunter. That means he's low-ranking in the clan. The lowest. Has to eat last and all that. But it turns out he's a gnaw wolf, or so they think."

"A gnaw wolf — what's that?" Coryn asked.

"Don't quite understand it myself. It's an art with them. They gnaw bones a certain way for the gnaw-bone mounds way out to the west where the Sacred Volcanoes are."

"Gnaw-bones? Volcanoes?" Coryn had never heard so many new words in his life. Well, he'd come for an education and, by Glaux, he was getting one.

"Don't know what a volcano is, laddie?"

"No, sir, I don't."

"Well, you see them mountains over there, spewing steam and fire? Them's volcanoes. The steam and fire comes out of the crater at the top." He paused. "Now, that's enough blather. I'm going down to pick what I can off this caribou. You wait a decent time, and after we get

76

a while at it ourselves, you can come down. I'll warn the other fellas you'll be coming."

"Thanks," Coryn said.

"Oh, think nothing of it. You see, laddie, everyone thinks that Beyond the Beyond is a lawless place. Well, it is and it isn't. A lot of outcasts come here that can't live in the civilized world. Thieves, egg snatchers, chick-nappers, murderers — hireclaws, you can buy them by the dozen. But we do have our way of doing things. You saw how them wolves brought down the caribou. That's a strategy. Wolves have the best strategies in the world for hunting. Never seen anything like it. I'd almost trade my wings to be able to think like a wolf."

Coryn blinked in surprise.

"Oh, yes, I would, laddie." The raven, or wolf bird, now lifted off from the rock outcropping. "See you at the carcass!"

CHAPTER THIRTEEN
A New Friend

It would not be the last carcass at which Coryn and the nameless raven would meet. But it was at the carcass of the moose that Coryn finally met Hamish, the gnaw wolf he had seen his first night in Beyond the Beyond. Hamish fascinated Coryn. The more he observed the lame yearling wolf, the more he realized that he was not only scorned by the others of the clan but was, in an odd way, feared as well. Then one day Coryn realized that it was not fear or scorn the other wolves felt, but that they kept Hamish in a strange limbo, feeling for him something between pity and reverence. In any case, Hamish was clearly an outcast like Coryn, and he wanted to get to know the wolf better. Coryn knew that he should not be distracted from his mission, which was to complete his education, to become a wizard like Grank of old, so he might help little Coryn reclaim the ember. But he was drawn to the little lame wolf, as well as being fascinated. So he followed the clan for just a bit longer.

The MacDuncans had been stalking a moose for the better part of a day and a night. After his last foray into the river, he could hardly make it up the bank, and that was when the wolves closed in on him. Again, Coryn watched that mysterious moment when the prey seemed to accept its fate as it locked eyes with the predator. It stirred him deep in his gizzard as it had the first time. After the kill the wolves ate and ate. It seemed as if it would never end. The ravens were getting hungry, and the wolves even allowed the birds to join them at the carcass, a rare event. Hamish, however, was still chased away.

Then, toward dawn, Coryn spotted a huge bear on the other side of the river. Phillip had once told him about grizzly bears, and from his description this one certainly looked like a grizzly. The wolves retreated quickly, as did the ravens. It was clear that they did not want to have anything to do with a grizzly, which could swat their heads off in a single blow.

But the wolves were not to be run off from their own kill for long. After all, they had stalked this prey for half a day and a night. Coryn was amazed when he saw the wolves keeping low to the ground, creeping up on the bear. There was a sudden explosion from the winter grass as six wolves pounced on the grizzly. Two snapped at its hindquarters, one went for its muzzle and tried to bite its nose, and two went for its belly. The sixth began barking and nipping. The bear spun and swung its immense paws. One wolf went flying from the blows, and the others scattered.

The bear went back to eating alone at the carcass. By this time, Coryn was starving. Dare he approach? He had an advantage, of course. He could fly off. He was just too hungry to wait another moment. He took off and hovered over the carcass. The bear took note of him but went back to eating. Coryn flew lower. This time the bear didn't even raise its head. The bear was working on the ribs of the moose, so Coryn settled on the hindquarters. He began to peck at the flesh. The bear continued eating without even giving him a glance. This went on for several minutes. He felt the wolves slowly creeping closer now, obviously emboldened by his success.

Coryn continued eating and, without turning around, spoke: "Listen to me, MacDuncans. Send Hamish in first and then the rest of you may come and join us," Coryn said in a tone he almost did not recognize. There was a strange calmness in his voice, like the stillness at the eye of a hurricane. He could sense the wolves laying back their ears and lowering their bodies in the signs of appeasement.

So the wolves stood back as Hamish came forward

and tucked in next to Coryn on the hindquarter. "I'm not used to this much meat. I mostly gnaw bones."

"So I've heard," Coryn replied.

Soon the other wolves joined them. They were careful to avoid the ribs where the grizzly was still eating and confined their own eating to the hindquarters, taking care to keep Coryn between them and the bear.

Occasionally, the wolves looked up, their muzzles bloody from their feasting, and wondered about the young owl. This had never happened before — bear, wolf, and owl feeding together — never in their lifetimes or in all the thousands of years that their kind had lived in Beyond the Beyond. And it all seemed the owl's doing. It made them nervous. It made them think of the old stories they had heard. It made them think of the Sacred Volcanoes to the west, still guarded by their clansmen. For that was where the Ember of Hoole, placed there so long ago by another strange owl, lay buried.

CHAPTER FOURTEEN

From a Distant Land

Far away from Beyond the Beyond, across the Sea of Hoolemere, a Spotted Owl made her plans in utmost secrecy. None of her closest friends, not one of the Chaw of Chaws, could know that this Guardian of Ga'Hoole, Otulissa, would make a journey alone — alone and somewhat uninformed. Otulissa did not mind the alone part, but she vehemently objected to her own unavoidable ignorance. It was no one's fault, really. No one knew of her mission except possibly the ancient Ezylryb. But Ezylryb was tight-beaked. One might more easily get a song from a stone as any information out of Ezylryb when he did not want to give it. And the same went for his ancient nest-maid snake, Octavia.

It had all begun in summer, and here it was now almost autumn. It had been midsummer when Otulissa had first begun sensing the scroom of Strix Struma. Strix Struma was her beloved leader and mentor, who had been killed by Nyra of the Pure Ones in a battle. And it was Otulissa in turn who had marked Nyra for life when she raked her battle claws across her face in sorrow and fury at her mentor's death.

Since the haunting by Strix Struma, Otulissa, who had not believed in scrooms before this, was driven by her inimitable scholarly curiosity to make a study of ghostly manifestations. She took from the library shelves a book she had never previously deigned to even look at: *Paranormal Activity in the World of Owls Since the Time of Hoole: Explorations, Case Studies, and Interpretations*. It was written by a certain Stronknorton Feevels, a Great Horned Owl. Otulissa had previously thought this was a pretentious title for a book that dealt in what she considered to be fake scientific phenomena. But as she read it, things began to make sense, especially when she compared it to her own experiences with Strix Struma's scroom. In particular, the book described a kind of mutism that seemed to afflict many scrooms, rendering them speechless at times when explanations were most urgently required. At the same time as the hauntings by Strix Struma, Otulissa had been involved in a deep study of the Fire Cycle cantos in the legends of Ga'Hoole. She had been prompted by Ezylryb to take another good hard look at the fourth canto, the meaning of which had always been considered obscure and controversial. She came to suspect that there was some connection between Strix Struma's scroomly visitations and the Fire Cycle, which told of the Ember of Hoole. She had previously thought that the Fire Cycle pertained only to King Hoole, but after several readings she began to suspect something more in it: that there was another king yet to come who would rule by the grace of the ember. It was a staggering thought. But there was no escaping it. And when the scroom had last come to see her, she had broken out of her mute state long enough to tell Otulissa that she must go to Beyond the Beyond, a journey that, in living memory, no Guardian of Ga'Hoole had ever made.

Nonetheless, Otulissa knew deep in her gizzard that she must go. What she must do once she got there would be revealed. For now, she simply had to fly on faith.

So, near the end of the season of Golden Rain, as the sun was rising and the great tree slept, she left. It was essential that her mission be kept secret. The Chaw of Chaws, her best friend, could not know. She had been picked for this mission by the scroom of Strix Struma. She flew to the cliffs on the far side of the Island of Hoole so that no one would see her departure. She had been preparing for this strange journey for nights on end — reading about wolves, studying their culture, the geography of the strange land. But as she spread her wings and caught the billows of salt air under her primaries, she felt a terrible loneliness. She missed her chaw mates. And the responsibility of her task weighed heavily. To this was added the uncertainty of the task itself. She knew she must go, but she still was not exactly sure why. It had to do with the Fire Cycle, the Ember of Hoole, and an owl who needed her help. The sun struck her wings and gilded the tawny feathers a bright gold. Resolutely, she banked into a starboard turn and headed off across the Sea of Hoolemere.

She anticipated arriving at Cape Glaux at night. She was a strong flier and would keep going through the night on a northwesterly course straight across Silverveil and the Shadow Forest. With luck, she would arrive at Beyond the Beyond within a few days. Glaux knew what she would do in that vast and desolate region frequented by hire-claws, dire wolves, and other desperate characters. She knew that no one was very social. Names were avoided for the most part. Good. She would not be bothered.

She had learned much about the dire wolves from Ezylryb's private library, which had a few very rare books on the creatures. The wolf clans were different — they had names and were social and highly organized, although they often fought among themselves. Dire wolves, however, had a strange code of conduct that required that they give sanctuary to any creature in need. Any wolf who broke this code by denying such sanctuary risked his life and that of his clan, for they would be set upon and killed by other wolves.

There was one more vital piece of information that Otulissa had learned in her extensive research, and that was about the Sacred Volcanoes where it was said the Ember of Hoole lay buried. The Sacred Volcanoes formed a ring and no one knew precisely in which volcano of the ring the ember lay buried. Mostly, the ring itself was guarded by dire wolves that were all descendants of the MacDuncan clan, but a few exceptions were made. Wolves from other clans could petition to become guards. These guards of forty or more wolves were known as the Sacred Watch. And most interesting of all, each of these wolves had been born with some deformity — a missing ear, a missing paw, or perhaps one blind eye. So it was only the deformed wolves from other clans that could petition for admission.

Because Otulissa felt that her mission to the Beyond had something to do with the Ember of Hoole, she thought it best to seek out the MacDuncans and ask for sanctuary as soon as she arrived.

Otulissa's talons finally touched earth in Beyond the Beyond in the very last sliver of a dwenking moon. She perched on the same ridge where Coryn had watched the wolves kill the caribou a few nights before and surveyed the eerie landscape. Although she saw no wolves, she heard their howls. She knew that wolves did not just howl at the moon, they howled to communicate information such as *a kill has just been made*, or *a herd of caribou is crossing the river*, or *I am hurt*. Another method of communication was scent marking, which Otulissa found deeply intriguing. Much could be communicated through their scent marks. With their highly developed sense of smell, they could amass nearly as much information about their environment as Otulissa might read in a book. The scent marks created a kind of map in their brains that very precisely defined the borders of their territory, where dangers might be, where a cache of food was, where others of their clan might be, the location of new open territories, and even possible birthing dens for pregnant females.

After reading about their extraordinary smelling powers, Otulissa regretted that those of owls were so inferior. What a help it would be to be able to sniff out danger, to smell ideas. She churred softly to herself as she imagined a library filled with books of not just written words but scents as well — *Smelly books! Lovely, lovely, all that knowledge pouring in through one's eyes, through one's beak, or whatever they call that thing that other animals have on their faces.* Oh, what she would give to be back in the library of the great tree at this very moment instead of this Glaux-forsaken place! She sighed.

"A sigh of regret or joy, madame?" A Masked Owl had lighted down on the ridge next to her. He was a Rogue smith. That much Otulissa could sniff. He had that ashy odor and his talons were blackened from working the fires with hammer and tongs.

"Just general weariness, I think," Otulissa answered.

"You're new here?" the Masked Owl asked. Otulissa narrowed her eyes so that the lids half obscured them. It was not a particularly polite gesture. But she was suspicious. She had heard that no questions were asked in Beyond the Beyond. She certainly didn't intend for anyone to know that she was a Guardian of Ga'Hoole. That would not be good at all.

"Permit me to introduce myself. I am Gwyndor."

Now Otulissa blinked in real astonishment. *What happened to the rule of no names?*

"I thought one did not give one's name here," she replied tersely.

"Some do, some don't. May I inquire as to your name?"

"You may not!"

He looked at her closely. Too closely. Otulissa was about to tell this Gwyndor to stuff a mouse in it and fly off. Otulissa hated owls and other animals getting overly familiar with her. Yes, she was snooty, she knew that. However, if this Gwyndor could help her with her mission, she would relent.

"I am in search, sir, of the MacDuncan clan," Otulissa said coolly. "If you could help me find them, I would be most appreciative."

"Ah, the MacDuncans. Yes, a fine clan, one of the oldest," the Masked Owl said. "They were hunting here a few days ago and then I heard they'd gone up into the region of the Pennvault River. That is their territory up there. So that's where you might find them."

"Well, that's very kind of you. Now, might you direct me to this territory of the Pennvault River?"

"I'd be more than happy to accompany you there."

"Oh, that won't be necessary at all!" She didn't want this sooty old thing going with her. He was shedding grime and fine ash over her lustrous white spots even as he spoke.

"Madame, it is no trouble, I assure you. I am going

there myself. I had heard rumors of an old friend of mine being with the MacDuncans."

"Oh," Otulissa said softly. She was flummoxed. What was she to do? It was a free country. An owl could fly anywhere he or she wanted to. Well, she would just not talk to him. Give him a bit of the cold feather, not out-and-out rudeness, but she would maintain a certain quietness that would suggest both dignity and mystery.

Of course, for Otulissa to remain quiet was almost a physical impossibility. She began yakking away as soon as they lifted off for the MacDuncan territory.

"Now, tell me about this smell business with dire wolves. What's all this scent marking about?" No sooner did Gwyndor answer one question than she popped out another.

"And do they use it offensively, would you say, or defensively? . . . And what about this elaborate code of honor, and yet they fight all the time? . . . You have an odd way of speaking, a slight, how should I put it?"

"Burr," Gwyndor replied.

"Yes, burr, that's it."

"It came with the wolves, from wherever they came from. They call the accent, in fact, the MacBurr."

"Oh, clever. But there is also a lilt that I detect. You see, I am quite an expert in languages. Linguistics is one of my favorite subjects. You know, I speak Krakish. Would you like me to teach you some?"

Will this owl ever shut up?! Gwyndor thought.

CHAPTER FIFTEEN
Violence in Silverveil

It's not so bad being "dead," Nyra was thinking as she flew through Silverveil. Glaux only knew how the rumor of her death got started, but it was serving her well. She remembered that dear Kludd had at one time been thought dead and it had allowed him time to rebuild his troops without anyone knowing. And that was exactly what she planned to do. Yes, Nyra had plans. Big plans. Now, having arrived in Silverveil, she was about to initiate the first stage of these plans. She knew that she could not keep up this ploy of being dead indefinitely. Quite the opposite. The first stage of her plan involved killing someone else. And the hammering from that someone's forge she could hear this very moment.

Her intended victim was the Rogue smith of Silverveil. Stupid creature had refused way back when to make claws for Kludd — she deserved to die. And once Nyra had gotten rid of her, she planned to assume her identity — to a point. She would not claim to be the Rogue smith of Silverveil, just a Rogue smith. She would take all that soot and ash from the forge and dust herself with it, particularly her face so that her scar would be covered. And she would take the bucket and the tools and head for Beyond the Beyond.

She was going to Beyond the Beyond with a definite shopping list: three Rogue smiths, four Rogue colliers, enough hireclaws for a battalion, and — this was her truly inspired idea — wolves! Dire wolves, to be precise, the largest, most savage wolves on Earth.

The idea had come to Nyra in the middle of the day, one of many restless days in which she could not sleep for her anger over Nyroc's betrayal and desertion. She could hardly believe she had never thought of it before. Why not enlist another species in the Pure Ones' battle to control the entire owl world? Hadn't the owls of the Northern Kingdoms done this years ago when they had used Kielian snakes and even polar bears in the long War of the Ice Claws? Well, this was getting to be a long war — she had fought St. Aggie's and she had fought the cursed Guardians, and she was not done yet. It was time to use a bit of imagination. The dire wolves could do just about everything except fly. They could run faster and for longer distances than owls could fly at a stretch, and they could swim equally well — and they were brutal.

The wolves were also known for their odd ways. Fiercely loyal, they had elaborate ranking systems within their clans that had to be strictly observed, not only by the members of the clan but by visitors as well. And she planned to be a visitor. For, in accordance with their strict rules of conduct, they were required to give sanctuary to any creature, no matter if that creature was the most Glaux-blessed soul on Earth or the most cursed outlaw. She must, however, come with gifts for them. Gifts for what they called the chieftain and his mate, in addition to gifts for the wolves just beneath him in importance, who were called the Noble Canis Lupus, whatever that meant. For these gifts she planned to go to Trader Mags in her disguise as a Rogue smith. She would bring plenty of trinkets to trade. Nyra had heard that the Rogue smith of Silverveil had ceased making weapons altogether and had turned to more "artistic endeavors." Stupid geegaws, just the kind Trader Mags would love.

Well, first murder, then shopping.

She was drawing closer to the forge. The whacks of the hammer and the sizzle of the fire camouflaged any sounds she was making in flight. The Rogue smith of Silverveil had set up her forge in the ruins of an ancient castle from the time of the Others. The forge itself was in a walled garden. Many of the walls had fallen down and offered excellent bricks for the forge. The Rogue smith herself lived in a cellar of the castle and that was where she kept her goods.

It was common knowledge that one never surprised smiths while they were working, as it could be dangerous for both parties. But that was exactly what Nyra planned to do, and she did not intend to get hurt! Only one owl was going to get hurt in this attack. She had her battle claws on; they were Kludd's and she took excellent care of them. She also carried a hickory club in one claw. She made one pass over and figured out her angle of attack. It would be steep. A classic death spiral used for going after medium-to-large prey. She began her descent, her gizzard trimmed for the kill, her heart beating wildly.

But just as she was ready to strike, the Rogue smith wheeled about. She held the tongs in one of her talons. She didn't seem surprised in the least. She quickly stepped aside, then lofted herself into the air. In her tongs was some ridiculous-looking creation that Nyra supposed was art. But art was no match for a club and battle claws. Nyra swung wildly. The Rogue smith dodged. *She is quick, this smith,* Nyra thought. She came in for another strike at Nyra, a feint to get her off balance. It didn't work. Now Nyra saw that the smith was trying to get to her hammer near the fire. Nyra could not let her get that hammer. The hammer would be much more deadly than the tongs. The smith was edging closer. Then Nyra had an idea. In a sudden direct rush, she flew at the Rogue smith, slamming her into her own fire. A terrible screech rang through the forest and the stench of burnt feathers filled the air.

Nyra grabbed the tongs that the smith had dropped and jabbed them into the fire, pushing the burning bird deeper into the forge. "They say, my dear, that the Guardians of Ga'Hoole enjoy their meat roasted. Perhaps we should serve you up there. What a surprise that would be for your sister, the famous Madame Plonk." Nyra shreed with laughter.

Now to the cellar where the Rogue smith kept her "art." Nyra found the smith's coal bucket and dumped everything she could into it. Then, before taking leave, she stopped once more by the forge. The Rogue smith of Silverveil was nothing more now than charred bones, and there were plenty of ashes. Nyra smeared herself all over — especially her face — thickly with the ashes, sure now that her scar would be invisible. Next, she slipped the hammer and tongs into the bucket. Nearby was a pond. She went to it to check her reflected image in the moonlight.

Well, now, if I don't look like a right fine Rogue smith, I don't know who does! Next stop, Trader Mags!

CHAPTER SIXTEEN

A Green Eye

Trader Mags, the magpie trader of fine goods and commodities, lived in a section of Silverveil that was particularly rich in churches, castles, and various old ruins from the time of the Others. It was the perfect place for her to find the stock of her trade. For years now, she had lived in the elaborate chapel of an ancient church. From the shards of shattered stained glass she made trinkets, and in the ruins of nearby houses she found old teacups and fragments of saucers. It was only a half night's flight to a fabulous palace that she had been ransacking for years, collecting remnants of old tapestries, silver goblets, and even scraps of paintings.

She had one of her favorite scraps propped in her nest in the chapel. It had been torn from a painting of an Other's face. It was just the eye. Mags found the Others' eyes fascinating and had torn several of them from various paintings. The eyes came in all colors, black, brown, green, a yellowish color that was not as bright as owls' eyes, gray, and the most beautiful of all — blue. She was hoping to find one someday that was red or purple. So far she had had no luck. Trader Mags herself was missing one eye. It had been plucked out by a crow many years before and this possibly explained her fascination with eyes. She wore a jaunty bandanna over it and she had learned over the years how to adjust her flying to her limited vision.

As Trader Mags sorted and re-sorted her goods with her assistant, Bubbles, she was thinking about revisiting the portrait gallery. She turned to Bubbles, a rather daft magpie, but helpful nonetheless. "Bubbles, it's a fine night for flying."

"Oh, yes, ma'am, that it is," Bubbles answered.

"I have meself a hankering to go to the portrait gallery looking for eyes."

"Yes, ma'am, and while you be there, it would be ever so good if you'd pick up some of them tassels from the curtains in the main saloon."

"Salon, Bubbles, not saloon. There be a world of difference between the two."

"Whatever!" Bubbles murmured.

"You mind the business while I'm gone, dearie. And remember the rules: silver for silver. No silver for glass. Actually, I don't want any more glass. We're up to our beaks in colored glass. And keep a tight talon on the eyes. Only trade them for something really good."

"Yes, ma'am."

"All right, tally ho!" Trader Mags loved this expression. Madame Plonk, one of her best customers from the Great Ga'Hoole Tree, had told her it was used by the Others in ancient times when they went riding on four-legged beasts. The owls of the great tree knew things like this because they could read, which she could not — or at least not very well. And Mags was fascinated with the lives of the Others, who had not lived on Earth for years. She sometimes wondered where and why they had gone, leaving all this great stuff behind.

It was not long after Trader Mags had flown off that Bubbles heard rather loud wings beats outside the chapel. She was surprised when an owl flew in. Usually, they were much quieter. She knew immediately that it was a Rogue smith. They often tried to trade coals for things.

Nyra awkwardly set down her bucket and the rest of the equipment she was carrying. Bubbles wondered if perhaps she had not been a Rogue smith very long, for usually they did not have such trouble coming in for a landing with all their gear.

"Got no need for coals. Sorry," she said without turning around from sorting stained glass.

"Oh, it's not coals I brought," said Nyra.

"All right, let's see it," Bubbles said, putting down the shards of glass.

"Much more interesting than coals. Is Trader Mags about?

"No, she went out on a business trip."

"Well, I've got some lovely silver things — not exactly useful, mind you. More like art."

"Oooh, art! Trader Mags, she does like the art," Bubbles said.

"How lucky, then." Nyra drew out a bright silver spiral-shaped piece.

"Ooooh, lovely. Melted down the silver, did you?"

"Yes. That was the easy part. Getting this shape was the hard part."

"Oh, yes, I can imagine," Bubbles replied. Trader Mags's words streamed through her head. *Silver for silver, no silver for glass.* "I suppose you be wanting to look at our silver collection."

"Not necessarily. Might I browse?"

"Of course. We got our glass over there, and our fine fabric fragments there. Beads, rocks there. Teacups." But Bubbles had hardly finished before Nyra had found a basket of scraps torn from paintings.

"These are interesting," she said.

"Oh, yes, Mags does like them eye paintings," Bubbles said.

"Oh, my goodness, a green eye."

"Yes, them Others, why, their eyes came in all colors, you know."

"But green, how unusual," Nyra said.

"Oh, sort through them, take your time."

"Thank you, my dear."

Bubbles thought how much more soft-spoken this owl was from most Rogue smiths, who tended to be rather rough in their ways.

Nyra remembered that the dire wolves of the Beyond were said to have green eyes. This would be the perfect gift. She began picking through the scraps and sorting out the green ones. After a bit she turned to Bubbles.

"Might I trade you my silver for these green eyes and, say, a bauble or two?"

"You mean, you just want some old painted eyes and not silver? It seems sort of unfair to you. Mags said we should trade silver for silver."

"Oh, don't worry about being fair to me, dearie. Just think of it as art for art."

"Well, yes, I suppose so." Bubbles paused. "I don't know. Mags is mighty particular about her eyes."

Oh, dear, Nyra thought. She hoped this magpie wasn't

going to be difficult. She didn't want to have to kill her. Then she had an idea. Flying with all this equipment was difficult. What if she would trade her the tongs along with the silver? "What would you say if I threw in the tongs?"

"Your tongs? But you need them, don't you?"

"Oh, I have more back at the forge. And quite frankly, I'm thinking of retiring."

"Well . . ." Bubbles cocked her head and tried to think this out. "I guess it's all right."

"Then, it's a deal."

"Yes, ma'am, it's a deal."

"You what?" Trader Mags shrieked when she returned from the palace. "You traded all my green eyes. I only had three sets and they took me forever to collect."

"And the tongs, we got the tongs, ma'am, along with the silver."

"Tongs? What kind of Rogue smith trades her tongs?" And then another thought burst into Trader Mags's head. *What kind of Rogue smith works with silver? Only one!* "Let me see that silver."

Bubbles flew nervously over to the church pew where she had put the silver spiral. She was certain that when Mags saw how beautiful it was, she would not be so mad.

"It's art!" Mags said when she had flown back with it.

Bubbles breathed a sigh of relief. "Yes, ma'am, that's what I say, art for art." But her relief was short-lived. Mags was shrieking again.

"There is only one Rogue smith who makes art, only one who lives near silver to melt down. And that is the Rogue smith of the Silverveil. She would NEVER trade this for a scrap of painting — never. You ninny! How could you not have seen that something was wrong? Something terrible has happened to the Rogue smith of Silverveil. I must go. Go right away."

"It warn't my fault, ma'am. Really, it warn't my fault!" Bubbles was crying as Trader Mags flew out of the chapel. "Be careful of crows, ma'am, do be careful!"

CHAPTER SEVENTEEN
Of Sky and Trail

Lochinvyrr." Coryn repeated the strange-sounding word. "So that is what you call it, that moment when a wolf and the dying animal look at each other."

Hamish nodded. "Our ways are odd, I know."

"It is odd, but it's beautiful. It's as if the animal is giving permission for its death."

"Yes, and the killer acknowledges that it is a worthy life he asks for."

"Asks. Not takes."

"No, we never take. And therefore the spirit of the animal we killed will follow the spirit trail of stars to the cave of souls in the sky."

"That sounds like our owl heaven. We call it glaumora. But it is just the sky, I think, and not a cave."

"You are a creature of the sky. So it makes sense."

And Hamish and his clan, Coryn thought, were creatures of the trail. He had never seen animals move as these wolves did, so swiftly. So steadily and never seeming to break their stride, even Hamish with his lame leg and his limp could run steadily for hours, although he was not the fastest of the clan.

"Is lochinvyrr another lesson you will teach the little Coryn who shall be king?" Hamish asked.

"I think it would be a good lesson," Coryn replied.

"Look, the clan is beginning to move. We should get ready." Duncan MacDuncan, the chieftain, had roused himself from the pile he slept in with his mate and their pups.

For several days now, Coryn had been traveling with the clan, for they had offered him sanctuary. And he was learning much from them. The wolves, like owls, preferred for the most part to travel and hunt at night and they often slept during the day. The caves they found were large, and Hamish and Coryn usually settled in their own little cranny toward the back because Hamish always stayed on the fringes of the clan. It was a useful arrangement. It allowed the two of them to talk privately.

The clan was as strategic about their travel formation as they were about their hunting. The traveling configuration was called the byrrgis. And the shape of this byrrgis varied according to weather conditions. The clan would string out if the wind was down and begin their trek with their tails slightly raised, their ruffs swept back. The females were faster than the males, so they were often in the front. But if the snow was thick on the ground, the males, who weighed more, would be in the lead to break the track. They would also be in the lead if there was a stiff headwind. In this way they could protect the fast runners from the wind, so that if there were caribou to be hunted, these females could put on a burst of speed unequaled by the males. The strategy of protecting the females and saving their energies for when it really counted was ingenious, Coryn thought.

He had seen this happen time and again. He was intrigued by the whole notion of the byrrgis and often wondered if it could in some way be used by owls.

He had learned a lot so far, but had he learned what he needed to teach a future king? And he had yet to see the Sacred Volcanoes. There was one subject that Hamish seemed reluctant to discuss: his role as gnaw wolf. Coryn realized that he, too, had been unwilling to discuss certain things. He had told Hamish how he felt it was his mission to come to the Beyond so that he could learn many things and become the teacher for young Coryn. But there was much he had left out. For example, he had neglected to tell Hamish that he had fire sight. He had betrayed no interest in going anywhere near the volcanoes. It would have been easy to fly high over them and look down into their fiery mouths. Why had he held back?

Perhaps he was frightened of what he might see. He was not even tempted to try his luck at being a collier and collect live coals from the streaming river of embers that poured from the volcanoes. And here he had thought he was going to be following in the footsteps of Grank, the first collier!

They had been steadily moving west, toward the ring of Sacred Volcanoes. Coryn was not sure why the volcanoes were considered sacred, but he did know that there were many gnaw wolves there. So he thought he might ask Hamish about the region. When they had settled down after their long trek, he noticed Hamish diligently gnawing on a caribou bone. He felt that this was the perfect opportunity.

"Hamish, are you practicing gnawing because we are going to this place?"

Hamish grunted a response, which Coryn took to mean yes but he didn't want to talk about it. Still Coryn persisted. "Hamish, can I look at the bone you are gnawing?"

"Sure, take a look." The wolf tossed it in his direction.

"Hamish, are you angry with me or something?"

Hamish sighed. "No, not you. I'm angry with myself."

"Why?"

"I'm not any good at this."

"At bone gnawing?"

"It's complicated to explain. Gnaw wolves lead strange lives. You see how I am not accepted, even scorned by my clan?"

Coryn nodded.

"Gnaw wolves are felt to have powers. We gnaw the bones with designs that tell stories of our history here. The gnaw wolves then pile these bones into huge mounds, or cairns, and these cairns — along with the gnaw wolves of our clan — guard the Sacred Volcanoes."

"Why do the volcanoes need to be guarded?" Coryn asked. But even as he asked, he felt an awful twinge in his gizzard.

"You really don't know, Coryn?" Hamish looked up, his green eyes seeming to bore right into Coryn's gizzard.

"No." Coryn's voice shook. "No, I really . . ." His voice dwindled off. *Don't say it. Don't say it!* He shut his eyes tight as if he could keep out the truth.

"They guard the Ember of Hoole," Hamish said in a low voice thick with the MacBurr.

There. It was out! thought Coryn. *Why do I keep resisting this?*

"You know," Hamish continued, "on that day when we first met at the carcass of the moose?"

"Yes," Coryn said.

"When you came that night and we all ate together, the wolves and the bear ate from the moose. Well, that had never happened before. Wolves, we're a superstitious lot. So talk began that your coming had something to do with the old stories. And because you befriended me, they now think it is my turn to go there, to leave the clan, and join the gnaw wolves who guard the ember."

"But it is a great honor, isn't it?" Coryn asked.

"Honors are lonely things. I would much rather have friends than honors."

"But I can still be your friend, can't I?"

"I don't think so, Coryn. The clansmen of the Sacred Watch have no friends. They pledged their lives long ago to Hoole."

"To Hoole?"

Hamish nodded. "Until the ember is retrieved, they are bound."

"But it's just a legend, isn't it?" Coryn asked in a quavery voice.

"Is it?" Hamish asked.

CHAPTER EIGHTEEN
Treating With the MacHeaths

With each step the wolves took and each wing beat of his own, Coryn felt that he was coming closer and closer to his destiny. And he was deeply frightened. He thought he had been sent here to become a teacher for little Coryn, but now he was not so sure. He remembered so long ago when Gwyndor, the Rogue smith, had told him that he had free will. He did not have to do this. He could choose. Mist had said the same thing. He could turn around and fly away. But to where would he fly? Back to Mist? She would be so disappointed in him. Back to Kalo and little Coryn? The Great Ga'Hoole Tree? Oh, how he longed to go there, but he knew that he couldn't. Not yet. Both Mist and the scroom had told him that there were tasks to be done. But what were the tasks? How did he have to prove himself before he went to the great tree, and why all of a sudden had his life become so bound up with Hamish's? Was Hamish going to the Sacred Volcanoes because of Coryn? Or was Coryn going there because of

Hamish? How had the Ember of Hoole bound them together? Hamish was to be its guardian but what was he, Coryn, supposed to be?

The land of the Sacred Volcanoes was in the farthest reaches of the Beyond. They were heading toward that precipice Coryn had imagined on his first night in the Beyond when he had seen the shimmering moon quiver on the edge of the horizon. For the wolves, the going was slow because there were great snowfields that had to be plowed through. Coryn had slowed his flight so as not to get too far ahead. Poor Hamish was always lagging behind with his lame leg. But Coryn noticed that the other wolves helped him more. Often they would let him eat first at a kill. It was obviously important to them that they deliver their gnaw wolf to his duty.

Hamish had told Coryn a little about the gnaw wolves' lives at this far edge of the Beyond. They were never allowed to mate or have pups. Their lives were solely devoted to guarding the ember. It was not an easy place to live and there were many dangers.

"It is the harshest weather in all of the Beyond. And the hunting is difficult."

"Hamish, how will you ever do it with your lame leg? You'll die of starvation."

"That is the curious part. All of the gnaw wolves who

go there suffer some sort of defect either from birth or injury. My leg is crooked. Another might be missing an eye or a paw. But something happens to them."

"What do you mean?"

"They grow stronger. If they are missing an eye, the vision in the other eye becomes sharper. Their hearing and their sense of smell are perhaps four times better than a normal wolf's. A lame wolf or one missing a paw develops muscles it never dreamed of and is able to run faster than any healthy female and break track in the deepest snow. They gather a strength unequaled while guarding the Sacred Volcanoes, and you shall see that they are huge."

"So what are the dangers, if they are this strong?"

"You see, there are other clans that would love to become the guardians of the volcanoes and the keepers of the bone mounds."

"Why, for Glaux's sake?! It sounds like the rottenest job in the world."

"Well, it is said that there are certain powers that the gnaw wolves gain throughout their lives of guarding the ember, in addition to becoming strong. And that the ember itself has certain powers.

"They say good King Hoole promised that in exchange for a life spent guarding the ember, after following the spirit trail of stars and resting for a while in the soul cave, a gnaw wolf's spirit could come back as anything it wanted to be."

"Anything?" Coryn asked.

"Anything."

"Do you believe it?"

"What else do I have, Coryn, but to believe it?" Hamish replied quietly.

"What would you come back as if you could? A bird? An owl? Maybe a fish?"

Hamish chuckled softly. "I would come back as a wolf born with four strong legs."

The trek was a long one, with the days weaving into longer and longer nights. But the wolves never broke their stride. One night as Coryn was flying overhead, he saw them halt to study something on the ground. Hamish split away from the clan and with his lame leg climbed painfully up a slippery trail to a promontory. He threw back his head and howled to summon Coryn, who had learned some of this strange, untamed music of the wolves.

He flew down and followed Hamish to the spot where the wolves were examining a paw print in the snow. To Coryn, it looked like an ordinary wolf paw print.

"Look at it hard, laddie," the chieftain said. "This is a dangerous sign. Here, compare it to my own print."

Duncan MacDuncan stepped back. Coryn dropped his head down close to the print on the ground. There was a difference, but he would never have noticed it if Duncan had not led him right to it. The four toe pads of the stranger wolf were much more spread out.

"What does that mean?" Coryn asked.

"Sick wolf. It is sick with the foaming-mouth disease. Wolves get it, but so can birds and many other animals. It drives them mad and they die. But the real danger is that their bite is like poison. If you are bitten by such a mad creature, you will also get the disease. We must travel very carefully now. And it is our duty to tell other wolves we meet that there is a mad one loose in these parts. You, Coryn, can be most helpful, lad, because you can see far and wide as you fly."

"Of course," Coryn said. "But what should I look for? My eyes are good but I don't think I could see a footprint like this from so high up."

"No, but you might see the wolf itself and you will recognize it quickly. Its stride will be broken and staggering. You will see the white foaming drool from its mouth, and you will hear its panting breath. Not at all like ours when we run. It is a harsh sort of breathing as if it breathes rocks or chunks of ice. It is a terrible sound. We shall be able to smell it even before you see it. But with your sight and hearing and our sense of smell, we shall know exactly where it is and be able to quickly change our course."

"Yes, of course. I shall help." Coryn was happy to be able to do something for this clan that had offered him sanctuary in this desolate land.

Coryn was not sure how many days and nights had passed since they had first spotted the paw prints of the sick wolf, but there did not seem to be others. Several times Coryn had flown wide of the byrrgis to look for the deadly wolf but had seen none that fit the description.

He began to wonder if he had missed something when he saw the chieftain and several of the nobles increase their scent markings and their sniffing. This slowed their progress even more. One evening at twilight, Coryn lighted down as he often did right on Hamish's back. The byrrgis had stopped and several of the wolves had gone out on scent-marking expeditions. "What's going on? Are there signs of the sick wolf?"

"No," Hamish answered. "We've entered the territory of the MacHeaths. They are a dangerous clan, but not as dangerous as the sick wolf. Remember, I told you that some clans are very jealous of the MacDuncans because of our clan being in the Sacred Watch of the ember? Well, the MacHeaths are the most jealous."

"Will there be a fight?"

"No. Duncan and his mate, Fiona, and McAngus will go and treat with them."

"Treat? What's that?"

"They will ask for a peaceful passage. They will promise them meat and hunting rights in our territory."

"Is it safe for them to go?" Coryn asked.

"There are certain rules. You cannot kill or attack another wolf if it is coming to treat. They will obey that, I think. And the MacHeaths, well, they are not highborn wolves. They are easily impressed and very superstitious as well. It makes them in some ways easy to deal with; in other ways it makes them very dangerous."

Coryn once again marveled at the complexity of wolves' lives and their clans. It made the lives of owls seem simple in comparison.

"I told you, Coryn, how a deformed pup's clan may petition for it to be a member of the Sacred Watch."

Coryn nodded his head.

"It's been said," Hamish continued, "that the MacHeaths so want to have one of their own become a member of the Sacred Watch that they have sometimes purposely maimed a pup."

"How horrible!" Coryn exclaimed.

"They are horrible. Very horrible."

Just at that moment Chieftain MacDuncan approached. Hamish immediately lowered his body, flattened his ears, and flashed the whites of his eyes. These were the immediate responses required of a low-ranking wolf when approached by a high-ranking one. Duncan MacDuncan gave a rough snort of approval. "I want to talk to Coryn."

"Yes, sir." Hamish seemed to grovel and lower himself more. This annoyed Coryn no end. He couldn't stand these cowering displays.

"Coryn, we are now in the territory of the MacHeaths."

"Yes. Hamish told me."

"Ah, yes." He gave a quick look at Hamish, barely acknowledging his presence, although Coryn continued to perch on the wolf's back. By Glaux, he wasn't going to move, either. Hamish was his best friend in all of the Beyond.

"We are going to treat with the MacHeaths. They are a difficult clan. But tradition dictates that we must request permission to pass through their territory. I would like you to accompany us."

"Me? Why me?" Coryn asked.

"The story of the bear and the wolves eating together after the owl lighted on the moose carcass has traveled widely. You are an owl that commands great respect. We feel that your presence at this gathering will be helpful."

Coryn blinked. He was amazed that the story had traveled so far and meant so much to the wolves. "My Lord Duncan," Coryn said, for this was the proper way to address a chieftain, "I am honored that you invite me to accompany you on this very important mission. It is the least I can do for the sanctuary you have given me."

Duncan MacDuncan then lowered his own tail slightly. Something a chieftain rarely did, for it was a sign of submission. In this case, Coryn took it as a gesture of gratitude. "We shall go at daybreak to meet them," he said.

"Not until daybreak?" Coryn asked.

"There is much to do before that."

Howling was what had to be done. The wolves of the MacDuncan clan formed a circle and began to howl. Their strange mad music laced the night. It filled the valley and skimmed over the mountaintops. They were answered back by equally untamed wild sounds. Then it ended abruptly as the sky began to lighten.

CHAPTER NINETEEN
An Eerie Feeling

Coryn had never been to what is called the Gadderheal, or the ceremonial cave of each clan. When he had first met the MacDuncans, they were far from their own Gadderheal. Hamish had told Coryn about them but he had not really known what to expect. Certainly not this. There was a fire pit in the center with coals brought by Rogue colliers or Rogue smiths. The wolves did not have skill with fire like the Rogue smiths or the Guardians of Ga'Hoole at the great tree but they liked it for their Gadderheals. Hamish had explained that in exchange for the coals, the Rogue smiths received killshares, or permission to share in the meat killed by the wolves.

Coryn was nervous about the fire. It had been a long time since he had been near one and he was not sure what he might see in the flames. He purposely took a place most distant from it. There were skins all around the cave from animals the wolves had hunted, and the chieftain and his nobles wore them draped around their shoulders.

The chieftain also wore a headdress of gnawed bones and teeth. Gnaw wolves who were not from the MacDuncan clan made non-sacred art from bones, and the chieftain's headdress was one such piece. There was also a talking stick, beautifully gnawed, that rested under the paws of whichever wolf was speaking.

"Welcome, Lord MacDuncan, to our Gadderheal."

Duncan MacDuncan lowered himself into the most servile posture Coryn had ever seen. In truth, he had never seen Duncan lower himself to any wolf. "We are deeply grateful for this meeting."

"And we, too, are honored that you have brought the owl. We have heard the stories of the bear and the wolf at the moose carcass."

Duncan MacDuncan nodded. "We have brought important news, along with presents as tokens of our respect and admiration of the MacHeaths."

"And what is this news, Lord Duncan MacDuncan?"

"There is a foaming-mouth wolf that skirts the edges of your territory. We have seen its signs. But so far we have not spotted it. Perhaps good Lupus," Duncan MacDuncan tipped his head back and up toward the sky, "has already taken it on the spirit trail."

All the wolves murmured some sort of blessing that Coryn did not understand.

"Thank you, Lord Duncan, for sharing this news with our clan. We are most grateful."

That had been Lord Duncan's plan. He was coming to ask for permission to pass through the territory because it was the most direct route to the Sacred Volcanoes, and he had brought presents, for which the MacHeaths would be grateful. But news of a foaming-mouth wolf was even more valuable. Duncan MacDuncan wanted this wily and cantankerous old chieftain in double debt to him.

"And now for the presents. Bring them forth, Sir Donalbain." An immense wolf with a gray coat brought forward a skin bag that he clutched in his mouth. When he dropped it in front of the chieftain's paws, several sparkling jewels spilled out as well as some finely crafted gnaw-bones from a famous MacDuncan gnaw wolf of old.

"He'll go for the jewels," Duncan had said before. "The old coot doesn't know a finely crafted gnaw-bone from a stick of wood."

He was right, for Lord Dunleavey MacHeath immediately started pawing the jewels. "Aaah, emeralds from the Emerald River. How interesting." He turned to one of his own nobles. "Sir Crathmore, will you fetch the gift our most recent visitor brought to us."

"Certainly, my lord."

The wolf returned in no time and set down a bundle of what looked like scraps of leather.

The wolves of the MacDuncan clan crowded closer to have a look.

"What is it?... Never seen anything like it." The MacDuncan wolves were puzzled.

"Art, they call it. Paintings. They are eyes of the Others, and all green at that!"

"Maybe the Others had a little wolf in them," Duncan offered. There was hearty laughter at this.

It was at precisely this point that Coryn began to have uneasy feelings in the Gadderheal. He could feel the heat of the fire and yet he resisted looking at it. At that moment, a scruffy wolf pup missing a tail lurched into the Gadderheal. It was obvious that the tail had been bitten off and, as Coryn looked more closely, he noticed that the reason the pup limped was because there was something wrong with one of his footpads. A sickening sensation washed through Coryn. He felt he might yarp a pellet any second, which he knew was not the thing to do in a ceremonial cave like a Gadderheal. But it was clear that, as Hamish had told him, this pup had been maimed on purpose so that he could become a gnaw wolf.

"Ah, Cody," said MacHeath, "our little gnaw wolf. Show Lord Duncan your bones."

Cody waddled to a corner and dragged out a few bones.

Coryn noticed a cream-colored female watching the lame pup and saw her then shift her gaze to him. He had never seen eyes brimming with such sadness. For a minute, she seemed to study him. Was she staring at his scar? *She could never know that I was maimed by my own mother, never!*

"He gnaws beautifully, as you see, Lord Duncan."

"Yes, I can see." Duncan MacDuncan could hardly conceal his disgust.

"His great-grandmum was a MacDuncan, you know."

It was in the midst of this conversation in which Lord MacHeath was obviously angling for the maimed pup to be considered for the Sacred Watch that Coryn, desperate to turn his eyes from the pup, caught a glimpse — just a glimpse of the fire. But in that instant he knew he could deny the flames no longer. He swiveled his head. He watched the flames first and then his gaze penetrated the glow of the embers. He saw a face, covered in soot, as black as a Rogue smith fresh from the forge. And beneath the ash and grime, glowing as fiercely as that moon perched and trembling on the edge of the Beyond, was an immense white face with a scar just like his own. He felt his gizzard grow still and then lock. *Nyra has been here! She has been right in this Gadderheal. She is the visitor who brought the green eyes as gifts.*

CHAPTER TWENTY

A Spotted Owl Goes Yeep

W hy didn't you tell me all this before, Coryn?" Hamish demanded.

"I couldn't. I just couldn't. I can't explain it."

Hamish thought a while and then said, "I think I can explain it. You have special powers. Fire sight, you call it. It's just like with gnaw wolves. Powers separate you from other creatures of your kind. Everyone thinks that to have power is wonderful, but we know it isn't. We know it's a lonely existence. We are both outcasts."

"Yes, exactly. But it is not just my fire sight that separates me. It is that my mother and father were the worst owls on Earth. They were brutal, horrid owls. This scar that you see on my face is the work of my mother's talons." Coryn thought this would shock Hamish but it didn't. "How would you like it if your mum did something like that to you?"

"Oh, she did something just as bad, far worse really, except she had no choice. It is the wolf law."

Coryn blinked. He had assumed that Hamish's mother had died giving birth to him, because there was no older female that he seemed to have anything to do with.

"You have a mother?"

"Oh, yes." Hamish nodded.

"In this clan?"

Hamish nodded again.

"What did she do to you?"

"When wolf pups are born, we are born naked and blind and deaf. We begin to hear within a few days, but our eyes will not open for almost eleven days. On the night I was born, when my mother saw my crooked leg and how ugly I was, she did not even lick off the birth sac but took me in her mouth and walked out into the cold night. She turned her head toward the highest ridge and began climbing. Never breaking stride, she slid through the night with her loathsome bundle. She put me on the ridge where the wolf birds would find me and eat me. My birth sac full of the juices and slime of birth might summon the wild cats that roamed or even the grizzlies. Or if I should wriggle enough, I might tumble down and crush my thin skull on a rock."

"How could she do that? That is so cruel."

"Not really. That is simply the way it is with wolves. If

the pup lives, that means it is marked to be a gnaw wolf and is taken back into the clan."

"And you lived."

"Yes, Duncan came to see if I had lived or died."

"So when you came back, did she nurse you?"

"She was no longer there, nor my father."

"But why?"

"It is a law: When a wolf gives birth to a deformed pup, both the mother and the father must leave the clan forever."

"Where do they go?"

"Some try to go to other clans. But news travels fast among wolves, and they are usually not admitted. No one wants wolves who give birth to deformed pups."

Coryn didn't say anything. But he did think that as awful as what Hamish's mother had done to him, it was not quite the same as what Nyra had done.

"Now, Coryn, the problem is that you, in fact, might meet your mother."

"Yes, it is a problem. More than just my problem. She's probably here trying to get hireclaws. It's her dream to rebuild the Tytonic Union of Pure Ones. She wants to control the owl world."

"Well, that might not happen." Hamish knew Coryn

was upset and decided to change the subject to one he knew his friend loved: the old legends. "They said that in the time before Hoole, the owl world was in terrible chaos. But when he came here to the Beyond and when Grank, the first collier, taught him how to dive for coals, he one day was seized by a vision. Some say it was the fumes from the volcanoes that gave him this vision, but suddenly he went straight for one of the Sacred Volcanoes. It was as if the volcano had turned to glass, and he could see right through it. He dived in and found the Ember of Hoole."

"But how did he not burn up?"

"No one knows. But when Hoole was dying, he returned to the Beyond and buried the ember. No one knows in which volcano, and for years after his death, many a collier died trying to dive for it. That was part of the gnaw wolves' job, to keep the wrong kind of owls away from the craters of the volcanoes. The volcanoes still attract colliers, because the rivers of coals have the kind they love, the bonk coals, the ones that burn so strong. And the colliers love to ride the she winds."

" 'She winds'?" Coryn asked. "What are they?"

"They are the hot drafts that come off the volcano. I

guess if you fly, they are considered a very sporting wind to ride. You'll see."

The first glimpse of the Sacred Volcanoes came at midnight. The Star Wolf, the wolves' name for the constellation that owls call the Little Raccoon, had not yet risen in the sky. But the sky itself was slashed with flames and the flames drenched the moon like blood. "It's like the whole sky is bleeding," Coryn whispered to himself as he perched on a very high ridge.

"Bleeding? An interesting word to use. Yes, perfect, I would say."

"Who's that? Who's there?" Coryn thought he was alone. He started to tremble uncontrollably. What if it was his mother? But it didn't sound like his mother. Who could it be? He was frightened. Should he fly or what? There was a cleft in the rock behind him, perfect for a young Barn Owl his size to hide in. He stepped backward and began to wedge himself in. *Not so perfect.* He really had to push himself in hard. He turned around and tried going in headfirst. He was sure his tail was sticking out. He then heard a nearby flutter. Something touched his tail.

"What in the name of glaumora are you hiding from? I'm not going to hurt you. I just thought we could have a nice little conversation. Creatures here are rather brusque.

Or let's just say they have not mastered the fine art of conversation. Now turn around, and let's have a little chat. I'm here on a mission — vague, I must say — not quite sure what — but give it time, Strix Struma said, give it time."

This owl sounded friendly enough and nothing like his mother. Her voice had more the sound of a Spotted Owl, if anything. And it was interesting that she, too, was on a mission and wasn't quite sure what it was supposed to be.

"Yes, I am on a mission as well and am a little bit confused about what it is I am supposed to do," Coryn replied.

"Turn around and tell me."

"Well, actually." Coryn churred a bit. "I'm kind of stuck."

"Would you feel that it was overly familiar if I pulled on your tail a little?"

"Oh, no, not at all," said Coryn.

"I'll try not to yank any rudder feathers."

"Don't worry, some are about to molt, anyhow."

"You're certainly a well-spoken young man."

Coryn didn't quite know what to say to that. "So, can you tell me a little bit about your mission?" Coryn asked.

"Oh, it's so nice to find someone interested in real conversation. It's almost like a code here — don't ask any names, don't ask about anyone's business or where they come from. So, yes, I'll tell you." She began pulling on his tail feathers, and Coryn felt himself budge slightly. "Now, don't think I am totally yoicks, but the scroom of a dear friend and teacher of mine appeared to me one morning."

"What?" Coryn wheeled around, freeing himself in the process. Could she be speaking of the kind old scroom who had haunted him and told him about the owl he was supposed to wait for in the spirit wood? The one who never came? The one called . . .

"Otulissa!" Coryn shouted. This was unbelievable. But then a terrible scream split the night.

"NYRA!" the Spotted Owl in front of him screeched. Her wings dropped and folded. She went into a yeep state and began to plummet from the ridge.

"Oh, Great Glaux, I've killed her!" Coryn exclaimed.

At that moment, a large Masked Owl intercepted the free fall of Otulissa.

"Pull yourself together, ma'am. Come on, get those wings pumping. Atta girl."

"I am not a girl! I am a commander of the Strix Struma Strikers and a ryb of the Great Ga'Hoole Tree."

The two owls had lighted down on a shelf that jutted out beneath the ridge. Coryn glided in quietly.

"Is she all right?" he asked. Then he blinked his eyes in amazement. "Gwyndor!"

"Nyroc, lad! Oh, Nyroc! You're here. I hoped you would come."

"Nyra!" Otulissa screamed again.

"No, no, ma'am," both Gwyndor and Coryn were now saying.

"It's not Nyra, ma'am. Can't you see he's a male not a female Barn Owl?"

"But the face . . . the face." Otulissa was hysterical at this point. "I put that scar there myself with my own battle claws in the Battle of the Siege just after she killed Strix Struma. I'd know that face anywhere."

"No, ma'am, you did not put this scar here. My mother, Nyra, clawed me."

Otulissa stared at the young Barn Owl and saw that, indeed, he was not Nyra. "Your own mother!" she said with a mixture of horror and awe.

"Yes," Coryn said, "when I tried to leave the Pure Ones. You must believe, ma'am, that I am nothing like my parents. And my name is not Nyroc, Gwyndor. I am now called Coryn."

"Coryn," Otulissa said softly and thought to herself how close the name was to "Soren." Indeed, once over the initial shock of his face, she saw a great resemblance to Soren in the young'un.

"But how did you know my name?" Otulissa asked.

131

"I heard it first in a dream. And then a scroom came to me."

"A scroom?" Otulissa said. Her voice was taut. "What did she look like?"

"She was old. A Spotted Owl like yourself. I met her in the spirit wood."

"In the spirit wood," Otulissa said softly.

"Yes, she said that we should wait for you. She said your name, Otulissa, and I remembered the name from my dream."

"Why were you waiting for me?"

"I think you were supposed to take me here to Beyond the Beyond. But you never came."

"I am sorry. I had doubts. And I think I was frightened, young 'un."

"Yes, I was, too," said Coryn.

And so here we both are, thought Otulissa. *Now what?* And she swiveled her head as if scanning the air for her old mentor, the scroom of Strix Struma.

CHAPTER TWENTY-ONE

Who's the Teacher?

"H e has fire sight, ma'am."

"You know that for a fact, Gwyndor?"

"Yes, I seen it meself when I did the Marking ceremony for his father. I could tell that he was seeing things
in the fire. I tried him a few more times and could tell
then, too. He saw the whole bloody history of his parents."

"Poor dear."

"And guess what else he saw?" The two owls huddled
closer. They had been traveling now with Coryn and the
MacDuncan clan. Coryn was roosting below with the
yearling Hamish in a small cave. But Gwyndor, knowing
of the superior hearing skills of Barn Owls, took no
chances. He had found a ledge far from that cave. One
could never be too careful around Barn Owls. So pressing
even closer to Otulissa, he whispered directly into her ear
slit. "He has seen the Ember of Hoole."

Otulissa felt her gizzard still. *Is this a surprise?* she
thought. When she had read that last canto from the Fire

Cycle that dawn, after the scroom of Strix Struma had appeared, the meaning of it had come to her in a whole new way, a new light. It seemed to be talking about another owl, not Hoole at all, as she had always thought. But someone else. The words of the canto came back to her.

> So bring him back with flames of gold
> Bring him back with burning fire
> For he reads what flames have told
> And his will is Hoole's desire.
> He shall not cease his endless flight
> He shall fly on through days and nights
> Though an outcast in despair
> He has a gizzard that is so fair.
> He shall return at summer's end
> With a coal in his beak
> A shadow king no more
> Tempered wise and brave for war.

Could that someone else be Coryn, son of Kludd and Nyra, son of tyrants?

"Does he know what his visions mean?" she asked Gwyndor.

"I don't think so. I think he sees things but he cannot always fit them together. I was talking to the gnaw wolf

Hamish, and he said Coryn thinks that he has come here for an education."

"Well, he certainly has, and I am to be his ryb, as we say in the great tree."

"Coryn doesn't see it that way," Gwyndor replied.

"What do you mean?" She narrowed her eyes.

"Well, first of all you must realize that the lad knows little of the legends of Ga'Hoole. The Pure Ones forbade such things."

"Yes, I would assume so. That would explain his ignorance."

"But he is not completely ignorant of them. He apparently has heard some fragments of the Fire Cycle and such. He knows a little about Grank, the first collier."

"Oh, dear," Otulissa sighed. "A little knowledge can be a dangerous thing."

"Yes, it can. Coryn seems to see himself in the role of Grank."

"What?" Otulissa seemed flabbergasted. "Has he ever done any colliering? Ever retrieved a coal?"

"Not that I know of. But, you see, he really sees himself as a teacher."

" For whom?"

"A little Burrowing Owl back in The Barrens who he believes is the true heir of Hoole."

"Where does he get these yoickish ideas?" Otulissa was genuinely perplexed.

"I don't know, but I only tell you all this because you're going to have to go carefully with him. Remember he believes that he's to become a teacher."

"But he also believes that the scroom of Strix Struma sent me to help in some way."

"Yes, that's true."

"How do you suppose we begin this entire undertaking? I mean, Gwyndor, do you believe that he is the heir of Hoole?"

"I am not sure. But I know that he saw the ember in the fire, I suspect more than once."

"Orf, the great Rogue smith of the Northern Kingdoms has fire sight."

"But there's a difference. Orf ain't never seen the Ember of Hoole. No. No owl has seen the Ember of Hoole since King Hoole himself."

Otulissa was persistent. "But tell me, Gwyndor, how do you know that Coryn actually saw it?"

"I can't explain it, ma'am. It's something I just know. Perhaps it is because I am a Rogue smith and I know how certain flames can well be felt in the gizzard. I sensed his gizzard lurching at that moment."

"Hardly scientific," Otulissa sniffed.

"It ain't science, ma'am. It be more like magic from the old times, the ancient times."

Otulissa was about to say that she didn't believe in magic, but a short time ago she hadn't believed in scrooms, either. And now here she was in this Glaux-forsaken place talking to this "old codger" of a Rogue smith because of a scroom. Otulissa sighed deeply. "Well, seeing the Ember of Hoole is one thing, retrieving it is another."

"Yes, ma'am. I think that is where you come in."

"Me?"

"Yes, you. You are known as one of the finest colliers in the colliering chaw of the great tree."

"Oh, you've heard." She lowered her eyes modestly.

"Yes, ma'am," he continued. "I've heard, and as you said, seeing the ember is not the same thing as retrieving it."

"But I can't teach him to retrieve an ember in the boiling crater of a volcano!"

"This young'un has never retrieved an ember from anyplace. You can teach him the fundamentals."

"You think so?"

"Ma'am, I know so."

"Well, I have heard that the south slopes of the volcanoes of the Sacred Ring are good for finding bonk coals and that the gnaw wolves of the watch permit colliering there."

"That they do. I'm no collier, but I've tried a bit of coal diving myself."

"Any luck?"

"No. Don't have the touch, ma'am."

"Well, let's hope young Coryn has it."

CHAPTER TWENTY-TWO
Basic Colliering

The most enormous wolf Coryn had ever seen was making its way toward them. He stood erect, his tail in a horizontal line with his spine, his brilliant green eyes staring at Hamish. Coryn would not notice until much later that he was missing one paw. Hamish immediately lowered himself, his belly scraping the ground, his ears laid back flat in a gesture of total submission. His lips were pulled in a grimace that revealed his teeth in a kind of grin that signaled complete obedience. Then Hamish lowered his head farther and twisted it so he was looking up at the higher-ranking animal. This final signal of appeasement was transmitted as he flashed his eyes white.

"Welcome, Hamish MacDuncan."

"My Lord Fengo, I am here to serve," Hamish said.

Coryn felt a current pass through him. Where had he heard that name "Fengo" before? Had he seen the wolf or the name written somehow in the fire? But he could not read then. He would not have recognized the letters. Yet he knew the name.

"And before you serve, you shall learn," Lord Fengo continued.

"I am your obedient student," replied Hamish.

"Your taiga is Banquo." Another huge wolf approached. He was missing an eye.

If Coryn had thought this land was strange, nothing could compare to the bizarre and extraordinary region of the Beyond he had now entered. There were towering bone cairns at intervals encircling the ring of the Sacred Volcanoes. They rose from glistening black beds of sharp grit, which was a kind of glass that the volcanoes' lava was ground into after years upon years. Atop each one of the cairns sat a gnaw wolf. And patrolling the space in between were other gnaw wolves. Hamish would begin his training period on the ground and then, when he was deemed ready, he would climb a cairn. From this vantage point, the gnaw wolves could keep watch on owls, look out for intruders. It was said that a gnaw wolf on a cairn could jump as high as an owl in flight and catch him on the wing.

"But what are they afraid of?" Coryn asked as he watched Hamish trot off behind his taiga.

"Well, two things, really. They don't want some yoickish

owl diving into the crater and losing its life, and ..." He paused and looked at Otulissa as if for help.

"Coryn, dear, they don't want the wrong owl retrieving the ember. An owl might come along who is Glaux-blessed with fire sight and sees in which volcano the ember is buried. But it is also possible that a vicious, tyrannical owl might try to retrieve the ember, and it would have to be killed immediately. The powers of the ember are too great for it to fall into dangerous talons."

"But how do they know if it is a good or a bad owl?"

"I don't know," Gwyndor replied. "They say it's in the gnaw wolf's bones — their own bones and the ones they gnaw for the cairns. It's a kind of code that has been passed down for centuries through the MacDuncan clan. That is why it is so important that only MacDuncans guard the ember."

Above them, owls wheeled in the sky, plunging to catch the edge embers, as they were called, that ran off the spills on the slopes of the volcanoes. There were other owls as well, mostly Rogue smiths hoping to strike a deal with the colliers for bonk coals. But the land was bleak and the dire wolves that slinked between the cairns did not have the easy camaraderie that Coryn had seen among the wolves of a clan. Perhaps it was because as young pups and yearlings, they had always been the lowest-ranking members, scorned yet feared, destined to always live at the edges of wolf society.

He already missed Hamish and wondered if he would be permitted to visit his wolf friend. He had not dared to ask when Fengo and Banquo has led him away. *Fengo!* Where had he heard that name before?

They were perched on a ridge now, and Otulissa had been observing the owls careening overhead, riding the hot drafty winds. She was saying that she had yet to see a bonk caught on the fly just as Coryn remembered where he had heard the name. It was spoken by the mystic rabbit in the Shadow Forest. The one who could find messages and visions in the designs of a spiderweb. The name "Fengo" had shown up in the web that the rabbit was reading, and she had told Coryn. The frustrating thing about the information in a web was that it never told the whole story. It seemed to Coryn that was always the way it was for him. He never got the whole story — not from the scrooms, not from Mist, not from the web-reading rabbit, and not even when he eavesdropped on parents telling the legends of Ga'Hoole to their young chicks before bedding down for the day. Always, either sleep or a squabble in the hollow would interrupt the storytelling, so Coryn would be left only with fragments. *Why am I here? What am I supposed to be doing? Am I really to be the teacher of a new king?*

"No, I'm the teacher," Otulissa's shrill voice blasted in his ear slit. He thought he had been thinking to himself but apparently he had said something out loud. "Coryn, have you heard anything I've said?"

"Oh, sorry, Otulissa."

"I was saying that not one of the colliers out there," she nodded toward the nearest volcano, "not a single one has caught a bonk coal on the fly, which is a shame. Bonk coals retain their strength if caught on the fly and not scavenged from the ground. Very inferior grade of bonk, ground bonk is. Am I not right, Gwyndor?"

"Oh, yes, ma'am, very inferior." *She's mighty picky,* Gwyndor thought. *I'd take any bonk coal, ground or on the fly.*

"But first we should start you with harvesting ground coals. Catching on the fly is very difficult. Now watch me scoop up a ground coal, and please note the position of it in my beak when I come back. It is called the 'Classic Grank Grip,' named, of course, for the first collier."

"Yes, ma'am."

"Now, before I lift off, I want to always check for wind direction." This was exactly what Otulissa now did. Then she circled overhead and called down, "You want the wind behind you when you begin to spiral in to collect the coal. You do not want the coal blown into your face. All right, here I go!"

Otulissa made a wide circle overhead, banked and turned, and began her spiral. She swooped in on a glistening orange coal bed at the base of one of the rivers of embers that ran down the slope. In no time, she was back with the coal in her beak. She faced front, then twisted her neck to the side and flipped her head almost completely around and back so Coryn could observe the Classic Grank Grip from all angles. After this, she dropped the coal into Gwyndor's bucket. "Sorry, Gwyndor," she sniffed. "Very inferior, class B, if that."

"Never you mind, ma'am. I'll take any bonk I can get." Otulissa gave the Rogue smith a withering look as if to say, *What's happened to quality these days?!*

"Now, Coryn, you try it. Remember all I said."

"Yes, ma'am."

"Wind check, then loose circle, steep bank . . ."

Otulissa kept talking as Coryn took off. But then just as he was about to pull out of his banked turn and begin the downward spiral to the ground, the volcano belched vigorously and a column of fiery embers shot high into the air. All the owls immediately began spiraling to earth to catch these hottest of bonk coals. All the owls, that is, except one.

"What in hagsmire is the young'un doing?" Gwyndor gasped.

"Coryn!" Otulissa screeched as she watched her pupil spiral upward at a dizzying speed.

Instinctively, he flew through the rain of coals, tipping his wings this way and that, catching first one coal on the fly in his beak, then another in his port talon, and then a third in his starboard talon.

"My Glaux," Otulissa gasped. "He's coming in fully loaded! Well, I never."

Coryn dropped all three coals in the bucket. The three owls peered into the glow.

"Magnificent," Otulissa said.

Three blue coals, with a flash of yellow in their centers. "Now, that is quality, Coryn. Those are bonk coals."

"I'll say so, ma'am. I should pay you for coals like this." Gwyndor was jubilant.

"Nonsense," Otulissa snapped. "Besides, I don't approve of accepting payment for coals from a sacred site. It's vulgar."

"Yes, ma'am, anything you say. Thank you very much."

"I need no thanks," Otulissa replied, and then turned to Coryn with tears in her eyes. "Seeing this young'un fly so exquisitely through that rain of embers is reward enough."

But what next, thought Otulissa, *what next? Oh, Strix Struma, you have brought us here. But what am I to do? The young'un still does not know himself. He does not recognize his destiny.*

Coryn was alone with his own troubling thoughts as he peered into the bucket.

Now what is that young'un seeing in those coals? Gwyndor wondered.

For Coryn, the coals in the bottom of Gwyndor's bucket seemed to breathe like living creatures. Coryn's fire sight was so powerful now that he did not need flames. The coals offered shapes and images as clear as the ones he read in fire. And what he saw first in these coals was the face of his mother, Nyra. And, as before, when he had seen her in the fire in the Gadderheal, her face was no longer white, but sooty and stained with smoke. There was a wolf figure near her. He wore a headdress of bones. *So she had been there,* Coryn thought, *or perhaps is there right now with the MacHeaths.*

Coryn felt the old fearful twinges in his gizzard exactly like the ones he had felt so often in the hollow he had shared with his mother in the canyonlands. But suddenly, his gizzard grew still. What was that deep in the coals? It flickered like the reflection of another coal. He blinked. There were only three coals in the bucket, but now each one was reflecting an image. The same image. It was orange, but at its center was a lick of blue and then around the edge, there was the green — the green of wolves' eyes.

This was not an image of a bonk coal. This was the reflection of the Ember of Hoole!

But where? How? What am I supposed to do?

You will know, Coryn. You will know, a voice whispered in his head.

Was it a scroom? Was it Mist?

When he lifted his eyes from the bucket, he saw Gwyndor and Otulissa staring at him hard. It was Otulissa, however, who shivered. "By Glaux, I felt as if a scroom floated by me." And then she churred a bit, as if to say, *Nonsense. I don't believe in such things.*

CHAPTER TWENTY-THREE
A Blood Oath

So I might stay as long as I care to, Lord MacHeath?" Nyra had just revealed her true identity. She had just told them that she was no Rogue smith but Leader and Supreme Commander of the Tytonic Union of Pure Ones.

"You bring us eyes that are green like ours. You hunt for the hare and share your meat and now you bring us what you have said is a great secret that could turn our clan into the most powerful wolf clan on Earth."

"Yes, but in exchange I need some information that you have," Nyra said.

"Sir Ross, take the talking bone to our honored guest, Nyra, Supreme Leader of the Tytonic Union of Pure Ones." This was a sign that Nyra was to give her information first. A black wolf took the bone and placed it at Nyra's talons. She clamped it firmly down with one talon.

"As the Supreme Leader of the Pure Ones, I would like

to propose an alliance between the dire wolves of the MacHeath clan, which I know number many, and the Pure Ones."

"And what is the purpose of this alliance?" MacHeath asked.

"To destroy the Guardians of Ga'Hoole and take control of the owl world."

"The owl world," the chieftain growled. "What does that have to do with us?"

"A lot!" Nyra answered.

"Please explain."

The next part of Nyra's proposal was based on a mixture of falsehoods coupled with many things she had found out about wolves and their ways in the Beyond. In the short time she had been in Beyond the Beyond, Nyra had visited many clans and had very skillfully ferreted out the dire wolves' strengths and weaknesses. She had listened to gossip. One rumor in particular had inflamed her gizzard. There was a young Barn Owl new to this desolate region that had somehow impressed the dire wolves with his special powers. She needed to know for certain who he was and, more important — what he was here for. The dire wolves would prove most helpful. She found out their grievances, discovered what was at the bottom of their endless feuds with one another. She studied their fears and hopes. The MacHeaths, she realized, were the most desperate of the clans and that was exactly what she needed. Desperate wolves, jealous wolves, who felt they had been cheated out of their birthright, their due, their power! She would offer them power even if she had to spin lies to do so. If she did it right, they would be unable to resist the temptation. So she began:

"As you know, the Ember of Hoole, which is buried in one of the Sacred Volcanoes, has been guarded for the ages by dire wolves of the MacDuncan clan."

"We know this all too well."

"And you also know that it has been claimed that the MacDuncan clan was chosen for this honor by King Hoole himself when he returned the ember to the volcano."

"Has been *claimed*?" A light flickered in the green depths of the chieftain's eyes.

"Precisely — claimed. In other words, it is hearsay."

"How do you know this?"

"Can you read, Lord MacHeath?"

"No," he replied.

"Well, I can." This was a lie. Nyra could barely read. Although she intended to learn as soon as she captured the great tree with its magnificent library. "I succeeded in infiltrating the Great Ga'Hoole Tree some years ago and read an ancient document that proposes that it was not the MacDuncans who were chosen by King Hoole but the MacHeaths."

"No!" There was a great growling mixed with yips and barks among the wolves in the Gadderheal.

"If you help me, I shall help restore to you what is rightfully yours."

"What is rightfully ours!" The chieftain's eyes blazed with such intensity, Nyra almost had to look away. "Madame Supreme Leader of the Tytonic Union, if indeed you can restore us to the Sacred Watch of the volcanoes, for this we shall join you and be forever in your debt."

Exactly where Nyra wanted them.

"Now, madame —" he continued.

"Madame General or General Mam is what I am accustomed to being called."

"Yes, Madame General. What information do you seek from us?"

"I have heard of a Barn Owl in these parts rumored to have unusual powers."

"Ahh, yes, the young one. Coryn, I believe, is his name."

"Coryn?" Nyra said. "Are you sure it's not Nyroc?"

"He was introduced to us as Coryn."

"He has been here? You have met him?" Nyra lofted off the ground into the air.

"The talking bone, Madame General. Mind the talking bone."

"Oh, I am so sorry," Nyra said and placed her talons once more on the bone.

"Our ways are curious, I know," Lord MacHeath said, almost apologetically.

"Can you tell me, Lord MacHeath, what he looked like and why he was here?"

"Well, I am not really sure why old Duncan MacDuncan brought him along. I suppose to honor us with his presence. You have heard of his connection with the wolves and the bear sharing the spoils of the moose." Nyra nodded. "Well, Madame General, that has never happened in the history of Beyond the Beyond since the time of Fengo."

"Fengo?" Nyra asked.

"Yes, Fengo was the first dire wolf to come here. Long, long ago he led his pack to Beyond the Beyond to escape the last Ice Age. In that time, they were called wolf packs and not clans. And the head gnaw wolf of the Sacred Watch of the volcanoes has always since been named Fengo to honor him."

A creamed-colored female wolf named Gyllbane looked narrowly at Nyra, her eyes becoming thin green slits. *There is something not right here. How could she not know about Fengo if she had gone to that great library? It was all written down.*

The entire history of the Beyond had been recorded, not just since the time Hoole came here with Grank, the first collier, but Fengo. Gyllbane shifted her weight and continued to listen.

"So I would imagine that is why Duncan MacDuncan brought him. To honor us with his presence. There has been much talk since the incident with the bear and the wolves that this owl has special powers of some sort. Some even say that he might be the true heir of Hoole and the one to retrieve the Ember of Hoole."

"This is most alarming," Nyra said. She hadn't meant to say it aloud, but news of the ember and what that meant to her plans had shocked her.

"It is, Madame General?"

"Well, we wouldn't want the ember to get into the wrong talons, now, would we?" Nyra recovered her composure.

"Definitely not, Madame General."

"And if this is the owl I am thinking of, well, it could be trouble. Can you tell me what he looked like?"

"Yes, he was a Barn Owl, as I said. A fairly large face for one his age and a scar that ran down it on a slant." Nyra felt her legs weaken. It was Nyroc. Nyroc in

153

possession of the Ember of Hoole — it was unthinkable. *What is the old chieftain saying now? Oh, what a bore he is and the whole cave stinks. Terrible gas these wolves have. Comes from eating that tough winter grass that grows here. Some sanctuary!* The old chieftain was still talking. Something about scars.

"You see, Madame General, we are most fond of scars. It is our own way of writing our history. We all bear great scars. Would you care to see them?"

"Oh, yes, of course," Nyra replied. *Good Glaux, as if this old dog weren't boring enough. Now I have to look at his scars.*

And it was not only his scar, a rather impressive one that raked down his belly, but the other wolves' scars, as well. "Ross here got that one in the skirmish with the MacDuncans; Edwidge lost an ear when he was ambushed by the MacMillans; and Gyllbane..." The creamy wolf trotted up to Nyra. "She got a nasty one on her shoulder in a ferocious fight with the MacAndrews."

Gyllbane looked closely at the owl. Beneath the soot, she saw a scar exactly like the one that marked the Barn Owl Coryn. There was something in the black eyes of this Madame General that she did not trust. But would Lord MacHeath listen to Gyllbane? He was stubborn. He rarely listened to anyone except his top nobles. She might have a nasty scar, but her rank was still low. Whose pup was it that Lord MacHeath had decided to mutilate in hopes of sending a gnaw wolf to the sacred watch? Her very own. How angry she had been. And she had to beg the chieftain to allow her to stay and not be sent away as was the custom when a female gave birth to a "deformed" pup. He had allowed her to stay but had run her mate off and forbidden any contact between her and the pup. Her own pup was nursed by a wolf in the whelping den while her own dugs hung heavy. How the resentment had built in her. She trotted back to her place in the Gadderheal.

While Nyra pretended to be interested in their scars, another idea had come to her. "Lord MacHeath, the scars you have shown me in this Gadderheal tonight only offer more proof that you are wolves of great valor. Wolves worthy to fight for a great cause. The news you brought me of this owl called Coryn disturbs me deeply. For I think I have heard of this owl from other parts of the owl kingdom. You should not rest easy, for is he not being given sanctuary by the MacDuncans, the very clan that has robbed you of what is yours? If, by some terrible quirk of fate the Ember of Hoole became his, think what this would mean for the MacDuncans." Hackles were raised and ears stood up. There were tense growls exchanged.

"And if this should come to pass, Lord MacHeath, I vow on my honor to set my sky hounds upon him, kill him, and bring the Ember of Hoole to you in this very Gadderheal."

A stunned silence fell upon the wolves.

"You mean that, Madame General?" MacHeath growled.

"My word is as solid as my gizzard."

Gyllbane raised a paw.

"Yes, Gyllbane?" The chieftain turned to the cream-colored wolf.

"The talking bone, if you please." A wolf picked up the bone and brought it to Gyllbane. She turned to Nyra. "This, Madame General, is a grave promise, one that could endanger you. It is most noble of you to do this." There was chuffing and growls of agreement. "A pledge such as this is usually undertaken with a blood oath." Again there were noises of agreement.

"By all means, fetch the oath bone, Lord Fleance," the chieftain ordered.

Lord Fleance quickly returned with a bone that had been gnawed to a deadly point.

More scars, Nyra thought. Well, she had been wounded in battle before. She could endure this scratch. The chieftain trotted forward. He was quick about it. Taking the oath bone in his mouth, he stabbed it quickly but not deeply into his front paw. There was a trickle of blood. He then dropped the bone in front of Nyra. It was finely honed, *sharp as battle claws!* If she could get these wolves to gnaw weapons like this! Nyra picked up the bone. Her hesitation was nothing to do with fear. There simply was not that much blood in owls' feet. But between her talons she might be able to get a few drops. She stabbed and a fair spurt came out.

Nyra and MacHeath then pressed talon to paw and swore an oath of loyalty.

"I, Madame General and Supreme Commander of the Tytonic Union of Pure Ones, do solemnly swear on the blood of my talons that I shall protect the rights of the clan MacHeath and shall pursue and kill the owl Coryn if he retrieves the sacred Ember of Hoole. And upon his death, I vow to return that ember to the Lord Chieftain of the MacHeath clan."

"And I, Dunleavy Bethmore MacHeath, Chieftain and Lord of the MacHeath clan, do solemnly swear to join in armed alliance with the Supreme Commander of the Tytonic Union of Pure ones, to aid and abet them in all of their battles as they seek to restore our own clan to glory. Their friends are our friends. Their enemies are our enemies."

"Hear! Hear!" All the wolves growled.

But Gyllbane hung back, for now she was sure of

something the rest had either not noticed or ignored. She was certain that the owl named Coryn was the son of Nyra. The resemblance was so great that she could not believe that the others hadn't noticed it. Perhaps they were too caught up in this owl's promises of restoration — yes, restoration and revenge could blind even a wolf's eyes. Not Gyllbane's, however. She knew that the owl called Nyra had just sworn by her blood that she would kill her own son. *What kind of owl is that? What kind of oath is that? She defiles the oath bone. There will be no honor, no glory for the MacHeaths.*

At that moment, the little pup Cody waddled in unevenly on his maimed foot pads. Gyllbane's eyes filled with tears as she watched him. *And to think he does not even know I am his mother.*

CHAPTER TWENTY-FOUR

A Gnaw Wolf in Training

Dunmore, Morgan, Hrath'ghar, Kiel, and Stormfast: These were the names of the five volcanoes of the Sacred Ring. As a member of the Sacred Watch, Hamish was being trained to learn the behaviors unique to each volcano. The periods of their eruptions, the fine distinctions of tone as well as the scents of the sulfurous steam that was spewed into the sky. When lava poured forth, which was seldom, he was learning to recognize what kind of lava it was and the course that the thick black roiling rivers would take down the steep slopes of a volcano. Most important, he began to learn from the older members of the watch the subtle signs that warned when any owl — Rogue collier or otherwise — approached the volcanoes with ill intent. They called such owls "graymalkins," a bad owl that might be making an attempt to capture the Ember of Hoole.

For his training, Hamish had been assigned to the south slope of Dunmore and at the very moment that Coryn had begun his spectacular flyby retrieval of bonk coals, Hamish's taiga had been crunching sheets of the black glass to familiarize the young wolf with that sound of alarm. "It will be louder, of course," Banquo was saying. "You hear the brittle sounds, don't you?"

Hamish was just about to say yes when a roar came from the owls around the south slope. Both wolves looked up.

"It's Coryn!" Hamish exclaimed as he saw his friend swooping through the storm of airborne coals.

"By my uncle's knees, look at that owl catch!" Banquo said.

The Rogue smiths on the ground had stopped haggling over the price of coal. The gnaw wolves on the cairns began to howl their approval, and the wolf birds squawked.

It had been a few days since Hamish had witnessed Coryn's amazing feat, and he had hoped that Coryn would come to visit, but so far he hadn't. The gnaw wolves of the Sacred Watch were not encouraged to socialize among themselves or with any creatures, for that matter. But Hamish had a feeling this rule might be relaxed in the case of Coryn. Banquo was very impressed that Hamish was the young Barn Owl's good friend. Hamish hoped that Coryn hadn't become too proud with his accomplishments to visit his lame friend, who was, in fact, getting stronger with each day. But he couldn't believe that Coryn would ever be that way. He was such a modest owl. So modest that he had not even tried to repeat the great feat. Hamish had not even seen him flying since that day. So he was somewhat relieved when he heard some other owls saying that they had not seen the young Barn Owl since the night of the triple-bonk catch.

One evening it began to snow. The she winds had died down and the red sparks from the volcano traced lazy patterns between the flakes as Hamish patrolled the trail between Dunmore and Morgan. He loped by two Rogue smiths who were swapping coals.

"I'll give you three of my best bonks for one of them you got in your bucket."

"Nay, them's the ones the young'un caught on the fly. He meant them for me."

Hamish slowed down. He recognized the Masked Owl Gwyndor, who was a friend of Coryn's from his earliest days. Coryn had told him about Gwyndor, and he had finally met him when they had all come here. But Hamish had not seen him since. He was anxious to talk to Gwyndor, but not while the other Rogue smith was around and, of course, it was forbidden when he was on watch. But he would soon be off duty. He only hoped that the Rogue smith would still be there. Why not circle back now and have a quick word, asking him to wait for him someplace? Yes, behind one of the piles of weathering bones.

The moon had only just begun to rise when Hamish rounded behind the bone pile. Gwyndor was perched on it.

"My, my," Gwyndor said. "Look how you've grown already. Look at that chest on you, lad."

"Yes, sir. What they say is true. This training does make one stronger."

"I'll say. Have you started practicing the leaping yet?"

"Just, sir. It's very hard. Especially being lame and all. But I guess I'll learn to do it."

"Sure you will, laddie. I tell you, there used to be an old gnaw wolf on the watch and he had but three legs. Well, one night, along comes one of them gray what-chamacallits — graymalkins. Oh, this was years ago. By Glaux, if that old gnaw wolf — Macbeth MacDuncan, I believe was his name — if old MacBeth didn't leap right up there in the sky and pull that old fiend down! But what did you want to talk with me for, lad?"

"Coryn. He's my best friend, you know."

Gwyndor nodded.

"And I haven't seen him for days, or at least not since the night he caught the coals on the fly."

"Aaah, yes," the Masked Owl churred softly. "Quite a night, wasn't it?"

"Has something happened to him?"

"No, lad. He just went off to have himself a think. He has much on his mind and his gizzard troubles him. He just needed a spell to think. But I'll be sure and tell him when he comes back that you've been wanting him to come see you."

"Oh, you will, sir? That would be ever so kind of you."

"Certainly, lad, certainly."

CHAPTER TWENTY-FIVE

From the River's Mist

Y ou must discover your own strengths, Coryn, your
own powers."

Ever since Coryn had made the spectacular retrievals of
the three bonk coals from the eruption, Otulissa had been
pressing him, but he was not quite sure what it was about.
She didn't seem to want to come right out and say it.

"Powers?" Coryn asked. "I don't have any powers." He
was hesitant to say anything about his ability to read
flames. Otulissa was nosy. She would want to know what
he had seen.

"Look at what you did, catching those bonk coals on
the fly, Coryn."

"Maybe it was luck. Did you ever think of that?"

"It was not luck. You flew those columns of flame and
coals like a seasoned collier. Listen to me." Otulissa stopped.
"No. What I really mean is, listen to yourself. Listen to your
gizzard and your heart, Coryn." Her yellow eyes grew more

lustrous. He could see in them that she wanted so much for him to understand something. He nodded slowly.

"Maybe I need to get away for a while," he said.

"Yes, that might be a good idea. Go where there are fewer owls and not all the noise of the volcanoes. I think it will help you," Otulissa said softly and patted his shoulder feathers with her wing.

Beyond the Sacred Ring, there was a river and it was here that Coryn had gone to think. He needed to be alone. Otulissa was nice, but she talked too much. And Gwyndor didn't talk enough. It was difficult to get an opinion from him. He remembered this from the first time he had really talked with Gwyndor back in the canyonlands. Ask him a question and he would always say something like "Oh, lad, I can't tell you what to do. . . ." Or "Laddie, in your gizzard you know the answer."

Well, Coryn didn't know the answer in his gizzard or anywhere else. But he had to think about the meaning of the reflections of what he had seen in the bucket of bonk coals. Yes, he had seen his mother's face, but he had seen something else, too — the Ember of Hoole. If he was the one destined to retrieve it, there were many questions still to be answered. First, how had he been so wrong in his thinking to imagine that the egg he had rescued, that of little Coryn, was a prince and that he was to be, like Grank, his tutor, his teacher? What was little Coryn if he wasn't a prince? Why had there been all those coincidences? Maybe he shouldn't be thinking about that right now.

Precisely, a voice said. But it was not out loud. It was in his head.

The scroom! He knew it! He looked toward the river from the rock where he perched. There was mist rising in swirls. It began to gather itself into a bundle with shimmering bright spots, a Spotted Owl. And through it Coryn could still see the falling snow. It was a most beautiful sight.

I thought you were nearby when I caught the coals. I think Otulissa thought so, too.

She did, but she almost denied me. The scroom spoke directly into Coryn's mind. *She is still embarrassed by believing in such things as scrooms. That is why I had to wait until you were alone. I cannot concentrate when there is even a speck of disbelief.*

I've seen my mother's image in the coals. She is near. I'm so scared.

I know, my dear. But you have seen much more, haven't you?

Coryn could not speak.

Haven't you, Coryn?

Yes, I have. I have seen the Ember of Hoole. But it can't be true that I am the one to retrieve it. Can it?

If not you, perhaps your mother, then?

Never!

You must make sure it is never. Not ever.

What was she saying? Why were owls and creatures always speaking to him in riddles? Why was it always scraps he got and never the whole answer?

There is no such thing as a whole answer, Coryn.

Is there truth?

One creature's truth is another's lie.

But can't I believe in anything?

Yourself, Coryn.

What?

There. I just gave you a whole answer, as you call it.

But it was just one word.

And you are just one owl.

But . . . but . . .

The scroom had begun to fade. *How will I know in which volcano to dive? Is it Dunmore?*

Suddenly, Coryn heard a sharp crack and then a rustle. Glaux, was it his mother? Had she stalked him all the way to this far edge of the Beyond?

CHAPTER TWENTY-SIX

In the Eye of the Wolf

Gyllbane had been on the trail for two days. She had slipped out of the Gadderheal the very same night after the "Madame General" had left. This was not a hard quarry to follow. She was one of the noisiest owls she had ever heard. Her wing beats were thunderous. She was, of course, heading for the Sacred Ring of volcanoes by the most direct route. It was getting on toward twilight of the second evening when Gyllbane first picked up the odd scent and then perhaps only seconds later saw the splayed footprint of a wolf. She stopped dead in her tracks. "Brachnockken." She muttered the ancient dire wolf oath and made a sign with her paw to ward off evil. She then sniffed some more. It was a wolf with the foaming-mouth disease, and he was headed in the exact same direction she was. She would have to change her course. The safest way, and unfortunately the longest, would be to follow the river. Would she get there before the owl, though?

Gyllbane had no choice. She simply had to. She was fleet, the fleetest of the whole MacHeath clan. It was the only reason the chieftain had allowed her to stay in the clan. Her speed made her not just a good hunter but a great hunter. If the snow was not deep, she could do it. She stretched out her legs, making long slicing strides. She gained speed. Her heart pounded. She would do this. She had only two thoughts. She would not let this mother owl kill her own son, and she would do everything in her power to destroy the alliance, even if it meant her own death. *I won't let this happen. I won't let this happen.* It became a song pounding in her blood, the rhythm of her stride, the cadence of her beating heart. Her ruff swept back in the wind. Her eyes were like two blazing green stars, her hackles were raised with the anger that coursed through her and drove her. On that night, she was the angriest wolf in the Beyond. She had all to gain and nothing to lose. She had lost her son. She had lost her mate. And she would lose her clan if she had to.

She stepped onto the ice to cross the river. If it cracked and she fell in, she could swim. She was as strong a swimmer as she was a runner. But the ice didn't crack until she got too close to the opposite bank. She fell in, but just for a second, and then clambered out onto the bank and rolled herself on the ground to dry. When she rose to her paws, she saw an owl. Not just any owl. *The* owl: Coryn, trembling on a nearby rock.

"I thought you were my mother."

Gyllbane blinked in dismay.

"Never mind. I heard the noise, and I was thinking about her and you scared me. I mean, I didn't really think you were her."

Gyllbane was panting hard. Never had she run so fast or for so long. "Your mother, the Supreme Commander of the Tytonic Pure Ones, she is . . ." She stopped to catch her breath. "She is coming to kill you. There is not much time. You must act fast." She paused to gobble breaths of air. "You must get the coal, the ember, the Ember of Hoole." Her breathing was ragged. The words tumbled out in painful chunks.

"Rest, rest just a little while," Coryn implored her.

"There is no time, Coryn. It all depends on you. She wants the ember. She has promised it to my clan, the MacHeaths. It will give them the power they have always been desperate for. In exchange, they will join her in an alliance to rule the owl world."

"But why are you doing this? You are a MacHeath."

"They took my son. They mutilated him. So badly did they want a MacHeath in the Sacred Watch, they cut off his paw pads and his tail. They drove my mate from the clan. How can I have anything but hatred for them? And if your mother succeeds, they will become more hateful and powerful beyond imagining."

"Cody is your son?"

She nodded. She was now drooling long silver strings of saliva, but she seemed to have recovered her breath. "Cody is my son but he does not even know it. I was not allowed to nurse him. But really, Coryn, there is no time. You must claim the ember. It is yours, I know it. I know it." Coryn looked deeply into her sparkling green eyes. His own reflection looked back at him with a steady gaze. Yes, there was fear in his own eyes, but there was daring as well. At last, he believed in what he saw reflected in that wolf's green eyes.

CHAPTER TWENTY-SEVEN
The Glass Volcano

In many ways, it was a night not unlike all the others. The Sacred Ring was wind-ripped once again. Red volcanic sparks and snowflakes were locked in a mad dance, blurring together to the music of the savage she winds that had returned in full force. On the ground, there was the usual bustle of Rogue smiths and Rogue colliers haggling over coals. The gnaw wolves of the watch patrolled their trails. The senior ones who were perched on the towering cairns of bones howled into the night a secret code of instructions, alerts, and commands that only they understood. A few of the bolder colliers were flying the higher and wilder layers of air in attempts to emulate the brilliant catches they'd seen Coryn make.

No one seemed to notice Coryn as he returned and began a wide circle in a survey of all the volcanoes of the ring. Gyllbane had settled herself in the shadows of weathering bone piles. She examined one closely. It was true these gnaw wolves were great artists. A wolf bird had been incised on the one she was looking at. It was perfect, down to the fine lines depicting its feathers. Would it have been so bad for Cody to be here on the watch? To become an artist, to become one of the most incredibly strong wolves on Earth and yet forbidden to mate, to be doomed to a completely solitary life without family or clan.

She looked up at the stars. Was it true what they said, that after a gnaw wolf of the Sacred Watch died and climbed the spirit trail, that wolf could return as anything it wanted to be on Earth? Would it be worth it? "No," she muttered to herself. Life is to live on Earth in the whelping den with your young, in the Gadderheal with wolves of honor, on the trails where the code of lochinvyrr is respected. That is how a wolf's life is to be lived. Damn the clan of hers, which kills and forgets the ways of lochinvyrr. Damn the MacHeaths for their jealousies, their mutilation of young pups, and their alliances with devil owls. She looked up and caught sight of Coryn. Slowly, so slowly, he was circling each of the five volcanoes. Other owls were beginning to notice him now. Many had stopped flying as if to make airspace for him.

Perched on a rock outcropping were two owls that had been watching him from the start. It was one of the few times in her life that Otulissa was completely silent. Gwyndor stood motionless, as if holding his breath. Both of their gizzards were in a frenzied state. They sensed what was coming.

Except for the screech of the wind and the occasional howl of a gnaw wolf, a hush had fallen over the Sacred Ring. This was Coryn's fifth circle of the ring. He could see Otulissa and Gwyndor watching him. He spotted Hamish on the ground. *He must be off duty,* Coryn thought, for he had stopped loping the trail between Dunmore and Stormfast. Coryn felt bad that he had paid such scant attention to his friend these past several days. He hoped there would be time later. He hoped there would be a later!

But despite this grim thought, Coryn was calm, as calm as he had ever been in his life. His gizzard was trimmed and fit for the challenge. Part of this challenge was patience. He knew someplace deep within his gizzard that it was not a matter of guessing which volcano the ember lay buried in. It would come to him in some inexplicable way and he would know *that one* is the volcano.

On the very fringes of the dark red shadows cast by the volcanoes, another owl lurked. If anyone had noticed her, they would have thought she flew most awkwardly for a Rogue smith. She set down her tools with a clank but no one heard it above the wind. Every creature's eyes were focused on just one thing: the young Barn Owl flying now for the sixth time over the top of the cones of the volcanoes — every creature, that is, except for the gnaw wolves on the cairns. Their hackles had risen the moment this other owl had arrived. A silent scent message went out. *Beware! A graymalkin is here.* Would she try to fly up where the young Barn Owl was circling? It could prove a difficult intercept if the two of them were fighting over the ember. Never in the history of the Sacred Ring had two owls attempted at the same time to recover the Ember of Hoole.

But the wolves were wrong. This owl would not attempt to retrieve the ember before Coryn. No, Nyra had it all worked out. She was not diving into some boiling volcano. Let Coryn do it and if he died, he died. He was no more the heir of Hoole than she was. But if by some freakish incident he did get the ember, well, then, she would wrest it from him. She would kill him and take the ember back to the MacHeaths. And if no one got it? Her plan would still work. She had promised to restore the MacHeaths to their glory as the true members of the Sacred Watch and then, with them by her side, she would begin to dominate the world of owls. *If only Kludd were here to see this. Kludd!*

Coryn looked down into the boiling crater of Dunmore. It was in Dunmore's cauldron that the bonk coals he caught on the fly had been born. And even though those coals had revealed to him the image of the Ember of Hoole, he knew in his gizzard that the great ember was not buried in that boiling cauldron. He flew over Morgan and peered in, and then Stormfast and Kiel. So far, he had been flying high, but it was as he approached Hrath'ghar that he noticed a strange phenomenon on the slopes just beneath the cone's opening. He began to hover. He blinked in dismay and now felt a quickening in his gizzard. The sides of this volcano seemed suddenly luminous. Now they were turning a pearly opalescent, and then the gleaming swirls started to glow and become translucent. Were the others seeing this, too? The night was strung with that wild savage music of howling wolves. Owls were flying in the lower levels around Hrath'ghar, but suddenly Coryn knew that they were not seeing what he was seeing at all. They had come to this volcano merely because he had been hovering so long. They did not see that the volcano was turning to glass!

And through that burning glass, Coryn saw the Ember of Hoole, orange with the lick of blue at its center ringed with green — the green of wolves' eyes. Just like those of Gyllbane! The ember was cradled in a black pocket of a lava bubble. Through the glass, he saw how the boiling lava sea grew still and the pocket in which the Ember of

Hoole rocked began to float to the surface of that black sea. Other embers, sizzling and popping from the crater, seemed to hang suspended for just a moment in the air.

Only Coryn could see this. This was the moment to seize. He spiraled up, high above the crater. Then, laying back his wings so they were flat to his sides, Coryn rocketed down into the crater. His last thought was *I have flown through the Shredders, I can fly through this*. He was amazed that he felt no heat within the crater and when he dipped his beak into the lava for the ember, it felt almost cool.

Like a fiery comet, Coryn whistled out of the crater. A blazing rainbow of sparks streamed from the ember in his beak. The wolves howled. The owls hooted and shreed and shrieked and crooned. Then the unique call of a Boreal Owl sounded like chimes in the snowy wind-ripped night, proclaiming: "The new king lives! Long live Coryn, Heir of Hoole."

The chant was taken up by all the gnaw wolves, wolf birds, and owls. Even a wandering caribou herd, which joined the braying in their own way: "Long live Coryn, the King!"

Otulissa, weeping, joined the chorus.

In the shadows, Nyra waited patiently. She said nothing. She merely glared, and because she was some distance from the rejoicing crowd, no one noticed her strange silence. But there was one owl who had been watching her since she had arrived. A great Snowy Owl. His name was Doc Finebeak. His white plumage blended in well with the surroundings. He had perched on a drift not far from where Nyra was. He wore a crow feather stuck jauntily among his back feathers. Known as one of the best trackers, he lived in the Beyond and, like hireclaws, had few scruples. His last job had been for Nyra, tracking down her errant son, who somehow had managed to fly through the Shredders to escape the Pure Ones. Ever since that job, he had vowed never to work for the tyrant again. His conscience had finally caught up with him that day on the far side of the Shredders. He had been shocked by her response when Nyroc, as he was then called, had survived. His mother had actually preferred that he die. Disgusted by the very sight of Nyra, he turned his gaze away. He looked across from where he perched to a nearby cliff and blinked. "By Glaux, it is Uglamore!"

He had heard that the former lieutenant of Nyra's was in the Beyond, that he'd deserted the Pure Ones shortly after Nyroc had escaped from the Shredders. The Guardians of Ga'Hoole didn't want him. He could never return to the Pure Ones, even if he wanted to. He was a marked owl as far as they were concerned, to be killed on sight. And this was where marked owls came. Doc Finebeak observed that Uglamore was certainly much the worse for wear. His feathers were tattered, with not a hint of luster. He was alarmingly thin. Just as Finebeak was looking at the old owl, Uglamore swept his head around and caught sight of him. The two owls locked eyes, then they blinked.

Uglamore had not seen Finebeak since the horrible days when Nyra had hunted down her son. Uglamore himself had always had a soft spot for Nyroc. And when he first heard that a young Barn Owl was in the Beyond, he had a hunch it might be Nyroc. Then he had spotted him that day at the carcass of the moose. He knew immediately it was Nyroc. The son resembled the mother right down to the scar he bore. He had heard a rumor that she had attacked him and scarred his face. So he had taken to following the young'un. Little did he imagine that it would lead to this. *Odd,* Uglamore thought, *that we are all now here together — Finebeak, myself, and the young'un, Nyroc.*

Uglamore had heard the rumors coming from the dire wolves that this owl was special — perhaps the one to retrieve the ember. But wolves were dramatic and naturally superstitious. He never paid much attention to their talk. But what he was now seeing was making him believe. This young Barn Owl, this fugitive from the Pure Ones, raised on hate and the vitriol of their vicious notions, this outcast of all outcasts, had grown noble. Here, indeed, was the true heir of King Hoole.

In that very same moment, Doc Finebeak was thinking the same thing. It was enough to bring a tear to a very cynical eye. And it would have if Doc Finebeak hadn't resolved to stay alert. He had to keep an eye on this female, the tyrant owl who was seething with such hatred, he could feel its heat through the frigid wind-whipped air.

She's going to make a move any second! I know it, Doc Finebreak thought. *And everybody's so drunk with joy they'll never notice it.* He looked around. He was going to need help to stop what Nyra was planning. But there was only Uglamore. As quietly as possible, Doc Finebeak signaled the old lieutenant to stay put — that he would join him on the ice shelf where he perched. Uglamore nodded.

When he lighted down beside the old raggedy owl, he whispered to him, "She's going to do something."

Uglamore nodded.

"She'll make a move soon. We have to be ready. Are you up to it?"

Uglamore nodded again. A grim fierceness burned in his eyes. It was almost miraculous. The old lieutenant seemed to grow young. "All right," he said.

Nyra spread her wings as Coryn began one more circle of the Sacred Ring with the ember firmly clamped in his beak. The colliers were flying madly below him trying to capture the sparks from it for their buckets. It was said that a spark from the ember ensured bonk coals in a Rogue smith's forge forever.

Coryn himself could hardly believe it. At this moment, his gizzard was brimming over with joy and something else — deep, deep gratitude. Until this moment he had never realized how many creatures he loved for the love they had given him — everyone including the beautiful cream-colored wolf, Gyllbane. He looked below for her now but couldn't find her. And Hamish and Otulissa and Gwyndor, dear Gwyndor who had hinted of such destiny but, more important, told him of free will. Yes, he had come here of his own free will. And Mist! Dear Mist. But right now he wanted to find Hamish and Gyllbane.

"Stop her!" he heard someone scream.

What was it? Coryn turned around.

Nyra!

"Come to Mama! Give it here!"

His gizzard screamed, *No!*

Coryn went into a steep spiral up, but then something caught his eye on the ground. A wolf was staggering near the edges of the ember beds. Sizzles went up as foam dripped from his mouth. *The sick wolf!* Suddenly, he had an idea. He spiraled down directly toward the foaming-mouthed wolf that was trying to bite its own tail.

"Look what the lad is doing!" Doc Finebeak said. "Brilliant! He's herding the old witch right into the jaws of the wolf with the foaming disease. Let's help!" Uglamore and he were off the ice shelf in a split second.

In no time, others picked up on Coryn's strategy. Hamish and Gyllbane seemed to come out of nowhere and began lurching at the sick wolf, driving him toward Nyra. Coryn was determined to keep flying low. If he flew low, Nyra would fly low. Everyone was joining in the attempt to drive the hated owl into the jaws of the sick wolf. They were in a fever. For eons, they had waited for a king, and now their young king was threatened.

Nyra did not quite know what was happening. She had thought it would be an air battle between her and Coryn, but she was actually being forced toward the ground. She wasn't a good ground fighter. *What's happening here?* She was now tightly surrounded. *Where is Nyroc?* Behind her were the biggest wolves she had ever seen. There was the cream-colored one from the MacHeath Gadderheal. *What is she doing here?* Nyra wondered.

"I'm on your side," she said in a desperate whisper as Gyllbane closed in on her.

The wolf's eyes glittered so brightly they cast a green glow on the patch of snow on the ground. "No, you're not! You're on no one's side but your own," Gyllbane said through bared teeth.

Nyra suddenly caught sight of the sick wolf. She could hear its rough breathing and see its foaming mouth. She realized now what they were doing as the other owls and wolves edged her closer and closer to him. She knew of this sickness. She knew it drove animals mad and that they died horrible deaths. She looked up for an escape.

"Uglamore, you old fool! What are you doing here?" she shreed.

"Watching you die," he replied in an even voice.

"Uglamore, you can't do this to me."

"Yes, he can," another voice said.

"Doc Finebeak, you'll help me, won't you?"

"Not on my life."

Above her, a phalanx of birds closed in, making escape impossible. Below her were walls of wolves and above them all, Coryn flew with the bright jewel of the Ember of Hoole clutched in his beak.

There had to be a way out of this. She hadn't lived this

long to die now. She knew every trick. She would figure out something. The wolves were strong and huge, but many of them were missing limbs. That's where the gaps in the wall of wolves would be. She scanned the legs. If she found a gap and was quick and flew low, she might get out.

But just at that moment, the sick wolf lunged. There was a flurry as all the birds and wolves leaped back to avoid the flying flecks of foam. One speck in the wrong place could mean death. But Nyra saw her chance.

I'm free! She spread her wings to rise, but Uglamore swooped down upon her. She tumbled sideways, stunned.

Uglamore! Coryn shreed silently.

It was unbelievable. The old lieutenant was now in the foaming jaws of the wolf. All eyes were on Uglamore and the disease-maddened animal. In the desperate confusion of the moment, Nyra flew off.

"He's dying! He's dying!"

Gyllbane charged the sick wolf, which dropped Uglamore's body on the ground, howled, and ran directly into the coal beds. In its frenzy, the wolf had thrown itself on its back and was now being consumed by flames.

The wolves and the owls had raced to Uglamore, who now was dying, for the wolf's fangs had stabbed right to his heart. "Stand back, stand back," Fengo, the chief of the

Sacred Watch, was saying. "You must not touch him. It is sure death."

Coryn now lighted down. The owls backed away from him. He did not carry the poison of death, but now seemed wrapped in the majesty of a king. Gwyndor came up beside him with his bucket and Coryn dropped the ember in so he could speak.

"Uglamore," Coryn whispered. "You took the fangs of the wolf for me."

"I took the fangs of the wolf for a king, Nyroc."

"They call me Coryn now."

"That is a fine name for a fine young owl."

"You left the Pure Ones. But why? I don't understand. You were one of Nyra's top lieutenants."

"When you hatched, young'un, I began to see things differently." He was gasping for breath now. His eyes rolled back in his head. "For a long time I doubted the beliefs of the Pure Ones. There is no ... aggg ... such thing ... pure is nothing. ... It is only the infinite and wonderful variety of owls that makes us rich. Barn Owl, Boreal, Snowy, Elf ... "

"Spare your breath, dear Uglamore."

But now the old owl had begun to foam at the beak and his body jerked in death twitches. The wolves looked on in wonder as their king crouched low to the ground.

Uglamore stopped twitching. He looked deep into Coryn's eyes, and Coryn looked deep into his. Around him, the wolves began to whisper in stunned voices, "It's like lochinvyrr, without predator or prey."

"Yes," said another wolf. "It's lochinvyrr between a king and his loyal subject who has died for him."

Coryn backed away from the body of the dead owl. "Rogue smiths," he said in a commanding voice that surprised even himself, "colliers, bring your coals. We must burn the body of this noble owl."

Within a short time, flames leaped up from the owl that was Uglamore. Sparks began to float off into the night. Gyllbane and Hamish came to stand beside Coryn. They tipped their heads back and howled. The other wolves joined in.

Coryn blinked. He could see the sparks arcing toward the stars.

"He goes now on the spirit trail of stars toward the soul cave in the sky," Hamish whispered.

"To glaumora," Coryn said.

"Yes, to glaumora," Hamish whispered.

When Coryn looked at his wolf friend, he blinked in disbelief. "Hamish, what has happened to you? Your leg is no longer crooked." He looked at the other gnaw wolves of the Sacred Ring. Fengo, the chieftain of the Sacred Watch, now had all four of his paws, and Banquo, who had been born without an eye, now had two glistening green ones. Wolves without tails had mysteriously grown them, wolves with misshapen hips now walked straight.

"What has happened?" Coryn asked, stunned by these transformations.

Fengo stepped forward and lowered his body in a submissive posture. He then put his head so it almost touched the ground and twisted his neck to look up at Coryn. Flashing the whites of his eyes, he said, "The Ember of Hoole has been guarded all these years. We waited for the right owl. Now the kingship has been restored. We are released from our duties at the Sacred Ring until, upon your death, the ember must be buried again. The prophecy of great King Hoole has come true, and after our lifetimes of service, we may choose to be anything we want or dare. We have all chosen to remain as wolves, to serve you, King Coryn, but we have also chosen to regain what we had lost. Our twisted limbs have been straightened. Our eyes are restored, our tails made whole once more. But we shall always be prepared to come to your aid, good King Coryn, always. That is our pledge."

"And I vow to protect you and lead you with all the

wisdom and fairness that Glaux has given me. To be mer-ciful and kind and just to all. To never fight for a wrongful cause. This I pledge."

Then all the wolves and owls on that edge of the Beyond, which swirled with sparks and leaped with flames, bowed down to Coryn. They had wanted him to wear a crown of finely incised bones, but he refused. Otulissa and Gwyndor watched from the side as Fengo urged him to take the crown.

"No, I need no crown," Coryn said good-naturedly. Then Otulissa began to whisper to herself the ancient words from the legends of Ga'Hoole: "And what was known of this owl was that he inspired other owls to great and noble deeds and that although he wore no crown of gold, the owls knew him as a king, for indeed his good grace and conscience anointed him and his spirit was his crown." She then turned to Coryn. "It's time for us to leave." Coryn blinked. A look of confusion filled his eyes. "To the great tree, Coryn." She gave him a searching look. "You know that is where the ember belongs now. And where you belong."

Coryn felt a joyous trembling in his gizzard as he never had before. It flooded through him. He felt as if he were shimmering inside. "To the great tree," he whispered. "Finally, to the great tree!"

Before he left the Beyond, Coryn sought out both Hamish and Gyllbane to bid them farewell in private.

"Hamish, you befriended me from almost my first day here. I shall never forget you as long as I live."

"Nor I you. But now you are king. Your Majesty."

"No, please, we owls are not like wolves. We do not have these complicated orders of rank, custom, and tradition. You must still call me Coryn."

"If it pleases you." But instinctively the yearling wolf began to lower himself to the ground.

"No, Hamish, please don't. You must be my friend first and always."

Coryn then turned to Gyllbane. "I see the sadness in your eyes."

"Does it show that much?" the wolf asked.

Coryn nodded. "You have now lost a child for no reason. There is no Sacred Watch for him to serve in."

"I have lost a child and a clan but gained a friend and a king."

"Would you not consider coming to the great tree? You are both strong swimmers. You could cross Hoolemere."

Both wolves shook their heads. "We are wolves of the Beyond, Coryn," Hamish said. "No matter what, this is where we belong. But if you ever need us, we shall come."

"Coryn," Otulissa called down from an ice perch. "We must be going."

"Good-bye, friends," Coryn said. They were all three weeping now. Coryn spread his wings and lofted into flight. Once more, he flew around the Sacred Ring with the coal in his talons and then, flanked by Otulissa and Gwyndor, he headed away from the star Never Moves, on a course south and east toward the Island of Hoole in the middle of the west Sea of Hoolemere where the Great Ga'Hoole Tree grew.

It was a fine night for flying. Coryn knew that although he was flying away from those he loved, he was at last flying toward something for which his heart and his gizzard had always yearned.

CHAPTER TWENTY-EIGHT

Uncle Soren and the King

A shadow had descended on the Great Ga'Hoole Tree. It was the shadow of death. The great harp had remained silent for days now. Madame Plonk's sister, the Rogue smith of Silverveil, had been murdered. And now Boron and Barran lay gravely ill.

"First Madame Plonk's sister and now this!" Audrey, one of the blind nest-maid snakes, commiserated with Mrs. Plithiver and Hilda.

"Oh, there goes Soren, I feel his wing beats," Mrs. Plithiver exclaimed. The nest-maid snakes were sunning themselves on this late autumn day in the time of the Copper-Rose Rain, when the milkberries turn their most gorgeous hues. It was usually a festive time, but not now. "I think he's on his way to Boron and Barran's in the parliament."

"Do you think the end is near?" Hilda asked.

All three nest-maids were silent. They didn't want to think about it.

Soren presented himself at the parliament entry. He remembered that when he first came to the great tree, he and the band — Digger, Gylfie, and Twilight — had discovered a place down deep in the roots of the tree from which they could eavesdrop on the parliament meetings. But he didn't have to do that anymore. They were all — Digger, Twilight, himself, and Gylfie — members of the parliament. He had been summoned here to the deathbeds of the old monarchs. This is where King Boron and his mate, Queen Barran, the monarchs of Hoole, had chosen to spend their last nights and days. Too weak to fly, barely able to eat, they said their time had come. They had been mates for life and they would now be mates in death, in glaumora.

It had shocked all the owls of the great tree when the two monarchs had become so ill at the same time. It was almost as if they had planned it. They were old, yes, but not as old as Ezylryb, who was still more or less flying. When Soren had been summoned, he had hoped for some sort of explanation, some clue as to why this was happening. As he entered the chamber, he was surprised to see that in addition to the band, the entire Chaw of Chaws had been assembled. All except for Otulissa, who was off on some mission. Soren was struck once again by how very odd it was that Otulissa was gone and by the way in which she had left — stealthily, at twixt time, without a word. They had learned about it only later, when Ezylryb had said that she was off on "some business." And he had heard that Nyra was raising a chick. But then, surprisingly, came rumors that the young owl had fled. Could Otulissa's business have something to do with that?

Ruby, Martin, and Soren's sister, Eglantine, were all present. Cleve of Firthmore, a healer from the Northern Kingdoms, motioned them forward to where the two monarchs rested, not on their usual perches, but in fluffy nests of down to which every owl in the tree had contributed breast feathers.

"Be brief," Cleve cautioned. "Do not ask too many questions, for they have much to tell you." The members of the Chaw of Chaws nodded.

"But where's Ezylryb?" Soren asked.

"You'll find out."

Surely he has not been sent out on a mission at this hour, Soren thought.

Boron summoned the Chaw of Chaws weakly with his talon. But it was Barran, his mate the queen, who first began to speak. Soren went forward slowly and with great apprehension. His gizzard had stilled. He knew what would happen soon. It felt strange. The passing of Boron and

Barran would mark the end of an era. The future seemed fragile. The tree would seem so frail without them.

"The first thing we want to say to you all," the old Snowy's voice was so feeble that they had to lean forward to hear her, "is that this is not a sad time. It is and shall be a time of great rejoicing."

The owls of the Chaw of Chaws were confused.

"Yes." Boron now spoke in a slightly stronger voice than his mate. "We see your confusion. But it shall be. Our dear Ezylryb is at this moment on the highest lookout branch of the great tree to welcome your new king — your true king."

"What?" all the owls said at once.

"What do you mean?" Digger asked. "You have been our true monarchs." Digger, the most philosophical of all the owls, could not contain himself. "What do you mean by the word 'true'? You have been most loyal and brave."

The two monarchs churred weakly. "Did I not tell you, dear, that Digger would question us when we said 'true leader'?" Boron turned his head toward his mate. She churred so softly it was almost inaudible.

"You are right. We have been loyal, but as king and queen we were not anointed in the way of that first king, King Hoole. We have been stewards, custodians, guardians of the kingship."

The two monarchs nodded feebly.

"But those tales of the ember and Hoole were just stories, just legends," Martin said.

Soren knew there was no "just" about it. Used like this, "just" was a terrible little word that snuffed out truth and possibility.

Boron's voice grew suddenly stronger. "It is through legends that our gizzards grow bold and our hearts strong. Legends separate the civilized from the uncivilized. A great thing is happening this evening. A prophecy is coming true. There is a young owl about to retrieve the Ember of Hoole."

Stunned silence fell upon the hollow of the parliament. Never had Soren expected this. Never in a thousand years. But then again, according to the legend, that was exactly how long ago good King Hoole had reburied the ember and then passed on to glaumora.

"At the moment the ember is his, we shall die. So it is writ." Barran's voice was growing more frail by the second. "Yes, you shall miss us, but do not mourn us. This is a great and happy occasion.... Our ..." She fought for a breath.

"Our business ..." Boron now spoke and in a thin voice finished the sentence, "on Earth ... is finished. Glaux bless you all." Both owls took one last breath and died. There was a slight wind in the parliament hollow as their spirits passed over.

The final ceremonies took place immediately. Soren returned to his hollow. His mate, a lovely young Barn Owl named Pellimore, or Pelli, was sitting on the clutch of eggs. Soren had rescued Pellimore from a fire in Ambala the previous summer. It hadn't exactly been love at first sight, because Pelli had struggled fiercely, thinking Soren was a Pure One. What had it taken to convince her that he was not? A recitation from the Fire Cycle. He would never forget her response. "Quite an appropriate choice, considering the situation we're in." Trees full of sap were exploding all around them. Soren had admired first her courage in trying to fight him off, and secondly her cool answer in the midst of the very hot fire. So their friendship began as a literary one. She knew the legends by heart, but she did not know how to read. He taught her, and she learned quickly. They spent many hours in the library together poring over books, and their passion for books had slowly turned into a passion for each other.

"Any action?" Soren asked upon arriving in their hollow.

"No," Pelli said and shook her head.

"Want me to sit for a while?"

"No. I want you to go figure out whatever it is that is bothering you."

"Why do you think something's bothering me, Pelli?"

"Soren, I can always tell when you're bothered. You have this odd little habit of fussing with your port plummels. Now tell me what it is."

"It's just that when Boron and Barran were dying, Barran said, 'At the moment the ember is his, we shall die. So it is writ.' But I can't find anything like it in any of the legends or the cantos. It makes me think that something is happening or about to happen."

At just this moment, Mrs. Plithiver slithered in. "Why, I think you're half snake, Soren, with your forebodings." Blind snakes were known for their refined sensibilities. "I have a feeling, too, that something very important is about to happen. The heat of that ember seems close. You two fly up to the crown of the tree. I'll nest-sit for you."

Soren knew there was no arguing with Mrs. P. or doubting her instincts.

"But Mrs. P.," Pelli protested.

"Quick, off that nest."

Mrs. Plithiver slid onto the nest and arranged herself in a wide spreading coil so she could cover each of the three eggs. How far they had all come together, she mused. The fir tree in the forest of Tyto seemed a lifetime ago.

Soren, a new hatchling then, had been pushed from the nest by his brother. *Now look at him, about to be a father of three little girl chicks.* Yes, Mrs. P. knew that in these eggs were three feisty little females.

Soren and Pelli joined Ezylryb at the top of the tree. It was a dark moonless night.

"Welcome," Ezylryb said.

"Good evening, Ezylryb, " Pelli replied. "Good evening, Octavia," she said to the fat greenish-blue snake that was suspended from a branch.

"How're the eggs coming?" Octavia asked.

"Coming, Octavia, coming," Ezylryb fussed at his old friend and nest-maid snake. "Eggs are completely boring until they hatch out, if you ask me."

"I didn't ask you. So, in your own words, why don't you put a mouse in it?" Octavia and Ezylryb enjoyed bickering. Even though they were owl and snake, they squabbled like an old couple, mates of the same species.

Soren was silent. His eyes were fixed on the dark horizon across the sea. There was something out there. A dim little pinprick of light. Was he the only one seeing it? He thought he could see colors. He spread his wings and lofted himself into flight.

"Soren, where are you going?" Pelli called out.

Ezylryb put a gentle wing on her. "Let him go. This is fitting, Pelli. He should be the one to greet him."

"Greet who? I can't see anything out there."

"But Soren does. He sees the first glimmer of the ember, as well he should."

Soren flew into the gusting winds. With each stroke, the ember glowed more intensely. It was a beautiful thing, just as it had been described in the legends. It seemed to draw Soren forward. He had never felt such joy coursing through him. He could now just make out the shape of the three owls. One was definitely Otulissa. One flew like a Masked Owl, and the third one in between them seemed to fly like a Barn Owl. Soren listened more carefully, contracting the muscles in his facial disk to scoop up the sounds. Yes, the heartbeat, too, sounded like that of a Barn Owl.

Closer and closer they came. The rest of the world seemed to fade away for Soren. The sea hushed, the winds died. He heard nothing except the wing beat of the Barn Owl. The Barn Owl flew so softly. It reminded him of the way his mum and da had flown years and years ago. That he could even remember such sounds was astounding. But the wing beats of this owl were identical. And then, at last, the owl's face was in view. First, he noticed the Ember of Hoole clutched in its beak, glowing beautifully in all of its orange and blue, yellow and green splendor. And then he felt a little jolt as he saw the scar running down the owl's face. But that was nothing. That was only the outside of the owl. When he listened more closely, he could hear the fine pulses of a decent gizzard, the beats not only of his wings but of a generous heart. And now Soren knew who it was. It was an owl born of tyrants, but with the heart and the gizzard and the mind of his grandparents. This was a noble owl.

Coryn dropped the ember into the bucket that Gwyndor held. Soren met them in midair and lofted down off Otulissa's starboard side. Otulissa spoke. "Soren, this is your nephew, Coryn, King of Ga'Hoole."

"Uncle Soren, I am honored."

Soren's eyes filled with tears as he dropped in next to his nephew and they continued to fly. "No, I am honored. You have done what no other owl could imagine doing. More miraculous even than retrieving the Ember of Hoole."

Coryn blinked.

"You who were born into evil found good. You who were raised in tyranny sought equality. You who were schooled in brutality learned only mercy. You who were taught the dishonorable discovered honor. You who were nurtured on the poison of the most ignoble owls in the world are most noble. You are my nephew and my king."

"And you are my uncle and my hero. But I still have much to learn. So I would also have you as my steward. You must carry the ember with me to the great tree."

Gwyndor then passed the two owls the bucket, and the king and his uncle flew forth.

As they flew on toward the tree, the owls perched in its limbs, waiting, saw a strange sight. Two Barn Owls flew toward them, each with a talon on a collier's bucket, but as they approached, the bucket seemed to become translucent as if it were made of glass. And the Ember of Hoole shined brightly through it. Indeed, the glow from the coal bathed the whole tree in its colors. It was as if a rain of embers had illuminated the entire island. Eglantine could hold herself back no longer. She flew out to greet her nephew and her brother.

"Welcome to the great tree, Your Majesty. I am your aunt Eglantine."

"Then I must call you aunt and you must call me Coryn." Eglantine blinked. "Yes, Coryn sounds fine to me. I might be king, but all my life, all I have really wanted to be is a Guardian of Ga'Hoole."

"Well, then, Coryn, come and follow me," Eglantine replied.

At that moment, Otulissa looked up and saw a gathering of glowing vapor in the sky. The spots shimmered brightly. She flew right up to her old leader.

"I believe, Strix Struma! I believe in you."

"Yes, dear. And what a fine night it is. It is a night for heroes and young kings. And now my business on Earth is finished."

"I believe . . . I believe . . . I believe," Otulissa kept whispering as she hovered, and the scroom of Strix Struma dissolved in the night to find her spirit trail to glaumora.

And all the owls of the great tree that night believed, as well. They believed that there were many kinds of truths, those of science that could be proven through the brain, and those of legends that could come true in the hearts and gizzards of all owls if they only believed.

"I am here," Coryn said in the great hollow that evening, "because there are owls who still believe in legends and the truths that can be found in legends, the truths of courage and loyalty, of goodness and mercy. My uncle repeated the legends many years ago when he was a captive in St. Aggie's. It saved him and my aunt Gylfie, if I may call you that." He turned to the little Elf Owl, and she nodded happily. "It saved them from moon blinking. It saved them from the destruction of the moon-blaze chamber. Where there are legends, there can be hope. Where there are legends, there can be dreams of knightly owls, from a kingdom called Ga'Hoole, who will rise each night into the blackness and perform noble deeds. Owls who speak no words but true ones. Owls whose only purpose is to right all wrongs, to make strong the weak, mend the broken, vanquish the proud, and make powerless those who abuse the frail. With hearts sublime, they take flight.... And I, dear Guardians, am an owl who was broken and powerless and weak, an outcast. Glaux bless you for your belief in legends."

OWLS
and others
from the

GUARDIANS *of* GA'HOOLE SERIES

The Band
SOREN: Barn Owl, *Tyto alba,* from the Forest Kingdom of Tyto; escaped from St. Aegolius Academy for Orphaned Owls; a Guardian at the Great Ga'Hoole Tree

GYLFIE: Elf Owl, *Micranthene whitneyi,* from the desert kingdom of Kuneer; escaped from St. Aegolius Academy for Orphaned Owls; Soren's best friend; a Guardian at the Great Ga'Hoole Tree

TWILIGHT: Great Gray Owl, *Strix nebulosa,* free flier; orphaned within hours of hatching; a Guardian at the Great Ga'Hoole Tree

DIGGER: Burrowing Owl, *Speotyto cunicularius,* from the desert kingdom of Kuneer; a Guardian at the Great Ga'Hoole Tree

The Leaders of the Great Ga'Hoole Tree
BORON: Snowy Owl, *Nyctea scandiaca,* the King of Hoole

BARRAN: Snowy Owl, *Nyctea scandiaca*, the Queen of Hoole

EZYLRYB: Whiskered Screech Owl, *Otus trichopsis*, the wise weather-interpretation and colliering ryb (teacher) at the Great Ga'Hoole Tree; Soren's mentor (also known as LYZE OF KIEL)

STRIX STRUMA: Spotted Owl, *Strix occidentalis*, the dignified navigation ryb at the Great Ga'Hoole Tree; killed in battle against the Pure Ones

SYLVANA: Burrowing Owl, *Speotyto cunicularius*, a young ryb at the Great Ga'Hoole Tree

Others at the Great Ga'Hoole Tree

OTULISSA: Spotted Owl, *Strix occidentalis*, a student of prestigious lineage at the Great Ga'Hoole Tree; ryb of Ga'Hoolology

MARTIN: Northern Saw-whet Owl, *Aegolius acadicus*, in Ezylryb's chaw with Soren

RUBY: Short-eared Owl, *Asio flammeus*, in Ezylryb's chaw with Soren

EGLANTINE: Barn Owl, *Tyto alba*, Soren's younger sister

MADAME PLONK: Snowy Owl, *Nyctea scandiaca*, the elegant singer of the Great Ga'Hoole Tree

MRS. PLITHIVER: blind snake, formerly the nest-maid for Soren's family; now a member of the harp guild at the Great Ga'Hoole Tree

OCTAVIA: Kielian snake, nest-maid for Madame Plonk and Ezylryb (also known as BRIGID)

The Pure Ones

KLUDD: Barn Owl, *Tyto alba*, Soren's older brother; slain leader of the Pure Ones (also known as METAL BEAK and HIGH TYTO)

NYRA: Barn Owl, *Tyto alba*, Kludd's mate; leader of the Pure Ones after Kludd's death

NYROC: Barn Owl, *Tyto alba*, son born to Nyra and Kludd after Kludd's death; in training to become High Tyto, leader of the Pure Ones: renamed CORYN after deserting

DUSTYTUFT: Greater Sooty Owl, *Tyto tenebricosa*, low-caste owl in the Pure Ones; friend of Nyroc since his hatching (also known as PHILLIP)

WORTMORE: Barn Owl, *Tyto alba*, a Pure One lieutenant

UGLAMORE: Barn Owl, *Tyto alba*, a Pure One sublieutenant under Nyra; deserts Pure Ones

STRYKER: Barn Owl, *Tyto alba*, a Pure One commander under Nyra

Other Characters

THE ROGUE SMITH OF SILVERVEIL: Snowy Owl, *Nyctea scandiaca*, a blacksmith not attached to any owl kingdom

GWYNDOR: Masked Owl, *Tyto novaehollandiae*, a rogue smith summoned by the Pure Ones for the Marking Ceremony over Kludd's bones

HAMISH: dire wolf of the MacDuncan clan; a gnaw wolf of the Sacred Watch; friend to CORYN

DUNCAN MACDUNCAN: leader of the MacDuncan clan of dire wolves in Beyond the Beyond

DUNLEAVY MACHEATH: leader of the MacHeath clan of dire wolves in Beyond the Beyond

GYLLBANE: member of the MacHeath clan of the dire wolves; her pup was maimed by Dunleavy

SLYNELLA: green iridescent flying snake of Ambala; companion to Mist

STINGYLL: green iridescent flying snake of Ambala; companion to Mist

About the Author

KATHRYN LASKY has long had a fascination with owls. Several years ago, she began doing extensive research about these birds and their behaviors — what they eat, how they fly, how they build or find their nests. She thought that she would someday write a nonfiction book about owls, illustrated with photographs by her husband, Christopher Knight. She realized, though, that this would be difficult since owls are nocturnal creatures, shy and hard to find. So she decided to write a fantasy about a world of owls. But even though it is an imaginary world in which owls can speak, think, and dream, she wanted to include as much of their natural history as she could.

Kathryn Lasky has written many books, both fiction and nonfiction. She has collaborated with her husband on nonfiction books such as *Sugaring Time*, for which she won a Newbery Honor; *The Most Beautiful Roof in the World*; and most recently, *Interrupted Journey: Saving Endangered Sea Turtles*. Among her fiction books are *The Night Journey*, a winner of the National Jewish Book Award; *Beyond the Burning Time*, an ALA Best Book for Young Adults; *True North; A*

Journey to the New World; Dreams in the Golden Country; and *Porkenstein.* She has written for the My Name Is America series, *The Journal of Augustus Pelletier: The Lewis and Clark Expedition, 1804,* and several books for The Royal Diary series, including *Elizabeth I: Red Rose of the House of Tudor, England, 1544,* and *Jahanara, Princess of Princesses, India, 1627.* She has also received *The Boston Globe* Horn Book Award as well as *The Washington Post* Children's Book Guild Award for her contribution to nonfiction.

Lasky and her husband live in Cambridge, Massachusetts.

Out of the darkness a hero will rise.

_____0-439-40557-2	GUARDIANS OF GA'HOOLE #1: THE CAPTURE	$ 4.99 U.S.
_____0-439-40558-0	GUARDIANS OF GA'HOOLE #2: THE JOURNEY	$ 4.99 U.S.
_____0-439-40559-9	GUARDIANS OF GA'HOOLE #3: THE RESCUE	$ 4.99 U.S.
_____0-439-40560-2	GUARDIANS OF GA'HOOLE #4: THE SIEGE	$ 4.99 U.S.
_____0-439-40561-0	GUARDIANS OF GA'HOOLE #5: THE SHATTERING	$ 4.99 U.S.
_____0-439-40562-9	GUARDIANS OF GA'HOOLE #6: THE BURNING	$ 4.99 U.S.
_____0-439-73950-0	GUARDIANS OF GA'HOOLE #7: THE HATCHLING	$ 4.99 U.S.
_____0-439-73951-9	GUARDIANS OF GA'HOOLE #8: THE OUTCAST	$ 4.99 U.S.

Available Wherever You Buy Books or Use This Order Form

Scholastic Inc., P.O. Box 7502, Jefferson City, MO 65102

Please send me the books I have checked above. I am enclosing $_____ (please add $2.00 to cover shipping and handling). Send check or money order–no cash or C.O.D.s please.

Name_____Birth date_____
—

Address_____

City_____-_____State/Zip_____

Please allow four to six weeks for delivery. Offer good in U.S.A. only. Sorry, mail orders are not available to residents of Canada. Prices subject to change.

www.scholastic.com/books

SCHOLASTIC and associated logos are trademarks and/or registered trademarks of Scholastic Inc.

■SCHOLASTIC

GGBKLST09(

THERE WAS A TIME WHEN LEGENDS WERE NOT JUST TOLD, BUT LIVED.

Guardians of Ga'Hoole Book Nine:
The Legends: The First Collier

In the first, stunning prequel to the bestselling Guardians of Ga'Hoole series, noble Spotted Owl Grank, the First Collier, discovers a magical Ember. When he's called to aid the king and save the royal egg, Grank hides the Ember so its power won't be misused. As battles rage, the fate of a kingdom rests with one lone owl.

📖 SCHOLASTIC

www.scholastic.com/guardiansofgahoole

Thrilling tales of adventure and danger...

Emily Rodda's

∽ DELTORA ∽

Enter the realm of
monsters, mayhem,
and magic of Deltora Quest
Deltora Shadowlands, and
Dragons of Deltora

Gordon Korman's

ON THE RUN

The chase is on in this heart-stopping series about two fugitive kids who must follow a trail of clues to prove their parents' innocence.

Gregor the Overlander
by Suzanne Collins

In the Underland, Gregor must face giant talking cockroaches, rideable bats, and a legendary Rat King to save his family, himself, and maybe the entire subterranean world.

Available wherever you buy books.

 SCHOLASTIC

FILLBO